Louis Kerkaldie

BUFFALO SEEKERS

A NOVEL
OF THE NAKOTA

BUFFALO
SEEKERS

A NOVEL
OF THE NAKOTA

by
LOUIS KIRKALDIE

FACE TO FACE BOOKS

Face to Face Books is an imprint of Midwest Traditions, Inc.,
a nonprofit press working to help preserve a sense of place and
tradition in American life.

For a catalog of books, write:

Midwest Traditions
Face to Face Books
3710 N. Morris Blvd.
Shorewood, Wisconsin 53211 U.S.A.

or call 1-800-736-9189

Buffalo Seekers
© 2000, Louis Kirkaldie

Cover design by MacLean & Tuminelly, Minneapolis.

Cover image is from a photograph by John Smart of Helena, Montana.
It depicts Middle Butte in the Sweet Grass Hills, a spiritual epicenter
for the native tribes, including the Nakota, that inhabited the region in
which this novel takes place. Photograph © 2000, John C. Smart.
Used by permission.

ISBN 1-883953-32-4 (hardcover)

ISBN 1-883953-33-2 (softcover)

for Naida, Kathleen, and Carla

The following pages were written to fulfill a promise to my children. As they were growing up, they were told many stories about their Assiniboine heritage and often asked that I write a story about these fascinating people who lived on the northern Great Plains of North America.

I was born in 1931 and grew up on the Fort Belknap Indian reservation in north-central Montana, home to the Assiniboine (Nakota) and Gros Ventre tribes. My grandmother was a full-blood Nakota, my grandfather was of European origin.

I attended an all-Indian school on the reservation through fifth grade, then we moved into the nearby town of Harlem when my two older brothers were of high school age. My father was on the elected tribal council for many years, and we took part in various tribal activities, attending powwows and occasionally the annual Sun Dance ceremonies (known in this book by its older name, the Medicine Lodge Dance).

After high school, I went on to college, followed by a career as a groundwater and engineering geologist.

The people of my grandmother, the Assiniboine, are a native people who in their language call themselves Nakota ("the generous ones"), or Nakoda ("the people"). Assiniboine is the name given to them by the Chippewa/Ojibwe, meaning

"One who cooks with stones," referring to an old method of cooking food by dropping heated stones into water to make it boil.

During the late 18th century, the Nakota had a population estimated at around 25,000 to 30,000, roaming the plains between North Dakota and the Sweet Grass Hills of Montana, south to the Missouri River, and north into present-day Saskatchewan in Canada (see map at right).

History books dwell on dates, battles, and famous people. The following pages dwell on the everyday life of the Nakota. I have tried to be authentic, as best I could, in writing about this way of life, based on my personal experiences, family stories, and historical research, but all of the individual characters in this novel are fictional.

I would like to give my heartfelt thanks to my wife, Jean, for her inspiration and editing, and to my daughter Kathleen Boas for her review of the manuscript and editing help.

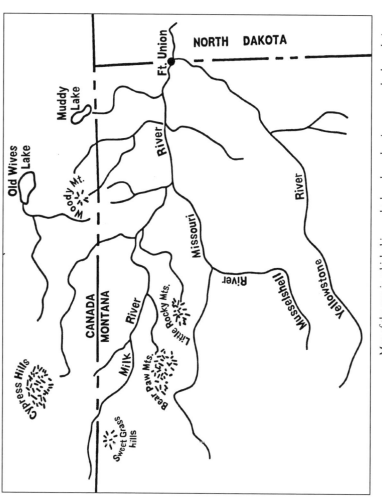

Map of the area in which this novel takes place, showing current-day boundaries.

CHAPTER 1

"Uncle, Uncle Stands Alone!" Walking Calf shouted as she ran toward the returning hunters. "Wind Walker had a baby this morning."

Stands Alone, twenty-one summers in age, sat very tall and straight on his gray horse. His dark eyes stared at the girl, and he flipped his long black hair over his shoulder where it made a striking contrast with his white buckskin shirt. His heart skipped a beat. Wind Walker was his wife of nearly two years. He wanted to shout, race his horse to his lodge, and hold his wife and baby in his arms. Instead, in the most calm and dignified manner he could muster, he asked, "What is it?"

"It's a boy, it's a boy!" she screamed, as she jumped up and down. Still mounted, the young man felt his heart begin to pound, and his mind moved so fast that he barely heard the congratulatory words from his fellow hunting partners.

As they came into camp, many of the children ran to meet them and see their kill. The pack horses, all six of them, were loaded with elk meat and hides.

Stands Alone's friend and hunting companion, Strikes The Ground, said, "Go and see your wife and new son. I will see to your horses and meat."

"Thank you, my friend. My niece, please go and help him

unload the meat and hides." Walking Calf looked disappointed, but obeyed her uncle.

Stands Alone dismounted very deliberately, trying not to show his excitement. He wanted to run as fast as he could to his lodge, but forced himself to walk slowly. A crowd of women, children, and a few elderly men gathered around the hunters. The women had knives and would help cut the meat to be shared in the camp. The young man looked back at the crowd and saw that no one was watching him. He broke into a trot, then a dead run for the last thirty steps. He stopped outside the lodge to catch his breath, and he could hear the voices of several women coming from inside. He slowly opened the lodge flap and entered.

Conversation ceased. He hardly noticed the other three women with his wife. Wind Walker was lying on a bed made of buffalo robes, the baby at her breast. She smiled at her husband, and her brown eyes beamed with love. All Stands Alone could see of his son was the top of his head. The baby made a crying sound, and Wind Walker looked down and smiled at the tiny bundle. Stands Alone thought his heart was going to burst out of his chest, and he fought back tears.

Blue Knife Woman and Old Fire, longtime friends of Wind Walker, looked at the excited father and smiled at each other. Blue Knife Woman said, "I must be leaving. My husband will be hungry soon, as usual." Old Fire agreed that she should leave as well.

The other woman, Feather In Cap, the village midwife, said, "Don't worry, Wind Walker, you will have enough milk for the baby, and he will be fine. I will go now so you and your husband can be alone with the child." As she stepped through the open flap she said, "I will be back later."

Wind Walker said, "Husband,* I am happy you are home. Come, sit beside me and see your son. He is beautiful." As Stands Alone sat down, she pulled the cover back from the pink body. Gently, she removed the baby from her breast and turned him over so that her husband could view his perfectly formed son.

Stands Alone put his arm around the shoulders of his wife, then stroked her long shining black hair which had been braided by her friends after the birth. With his other hand he took the baby's delicate hand and said, "Welcome to our world, my son."

And to Wind Walker he said, "My love for you is greater now than ever." Tears filled his eyes, and he looked away. Wind Walker caressed the arm of her husband and patted his back. They both watched the baby as it moved.

"Look, husband, the baby is smiling at you."

The umbilical cord was the only evidence left that indicated that the boy had been born just that morning. It had been carefully tied and severed with a sharp, short-bladed knife which the midwife kept for that purpose only. Later, when the cord completely dried, Wind Walker would take what remained and place it, along with some tobacco, in a small pouch. This diamond-shaped buckskin pouch, about the size of the newborn babe's hand, was decorated with dyed porcupine quills. It would be kept by the mother as a reminder of the bond of intimacy that had been shared between mother and child.

The baby began to cry. Wind Walker said, "He is hungry again," and turned him back to her breast. She smiled at her

. . . .

* Husbands and wives never called each other by their names.

husband as their son made the noises of suckling.

Stands Alone watched as the baby fed, and Wind Walker said, "Blue Knife Woman is our son's sponsor. She came and took the boy as soon as he was born, cleaned his mouth, and washed his body. She is a fine woman with a strong will, and has much fun in life. Our son will inherit her good qualities." This was very important – that a woman with good character agreed to perform the duties of sponsor. Before cleaning the baby after birth, such a woman must look carefully into her own inner nature, because the child would inherit her type of personality.

"Everyone knows her as a good woman," agreed Stands Alone. "I am happy for the boy. He is fortunate that she was present."

"The Boy," as their son would be called until a formal naming ceremony, stopped the sucking noises, and soon was asleep. His mother gently lifted him from her breast and put him into a cradle she had made of soft white buckskin. Wind Walker had elaborately decorated this sleeping bag with dyed porcupine quills of many colors. Also, a few of the white man's beads were sewn along the edge of the opening that surrounded the face of the baby.

The cradle could be laced from bottom to top, and was portable so the child could be carried anywhere the mother went. The lower part of the bag was filled with the fluffed soft, downy, ripe cattails – these served as both blanket and diaper. They could be removed and the supply renewed as needed.

With tears in her eyes, Wind Walker looked at the baby, then at her husband. She said, "There is only one thing that could make me happier, and that would be to share our son with our mothers and fathers – if they were still alive."

Stands Alone put his arms around his wife, held her gently and caressed her hair. His eyes, too, became clouded with tears. His memory soared in an instant back to that black summer five years past when a great number of his tribe, the Nakota, including his parents, had died of smallpox.

"My love, I have the same feelings in my heart." He then rose and slowly moved to the lodge entrance. According to custom, this door flap always faced south.

As he stepped from the lodge, Stands Alone could see several children playing beside the stream near the encampment. Big Warm Creek was so named because it issued from a large, very warm spring at the base of the Little Rocky Mountains, a short ride to the west.

The man turned to the east and saw the narrow canyon in the pine ridge through which the hunters had brought their kill that day. He then turned toward the jewel-like island mountains which seemed to have been thrust out of the surrounding plains. The sun was beginning to set behind the heights, and the peaks appeared dusky and mysterious.

As he stood silently in the fading light, his heart flooding with emotion at the birth of his son, the crimson sky carried him away to the memory of his dead parents.

CHAPTER 2

The frightened, emaciated man fell from his exhausted horse. Several men from the village ran to help him. He waved them away, and in barely a whisper, said, "Do not touch me. Stay away. Do not come near or you will die."

Sixteen years of age at the time, Stands Alone stared at the man and backed away. The poor fellow's face and throat were swollen, and red spots covering his body oozed a yellowish substance. The stricken man was hardly recognizable. Then Stands Alone noticed a familiar design on the man's shirt and realized it was none other than Buffalo Calf, an older man from his own village, about three days' ride to the north.

Stands Alone and the dying man were part of the Little Rock Mountain Band of the Nakota. After the Medicine Lodge Dance, held during the first full moon after the summer equinox, the band had split in two. About sixty lodges, including Stands Alone's family, moved north and west along the Milk River. The remaining lodges, about fifty in number, moved south near the Little Rocky Mountains. With permission from his father, Stands Alone had remained for most of the summer with the latter group, visiting friends and relatives.

Buffalo Calf had grown up with Stands Alone's father. They had been boyhood companions, and later hunted together, and fought the Piegans, part of the Blackfeet tribe who lived far to the west. At one time this man had saved the life of Stands Alone's father. They had raided the camp of the Piegans and stolen two dozen horses. As they raced out of the camp in the early morning light, the mount of Stands Alone's father fell. The horse rolled over and broke the rider's leg. Buffalo Calf had raced to his aid and lifted his injured friend onto his own mount. He then jumped up behind, and riding double, they galloped away before they could be killed by the Piegans who were pursuing on foot. They had been welcomed as great warriors two days later when they arrived back at their camp.

As Stands Alone recalled that incident, one of the village soldiers who helped keep order in the camp came up, looked at the terrible sight of the afflicted Buffalo Calf, and asked, "What happened? Why are you sick?" He quickly called for someone to go and bring the medicine man.

With great effort and power of will, the weakened man began to tell the dark story of many friends and relatives suffering the horrible death which smallpox brings. Old men, old women, babies, young mothers, strong warriors, boys, and girls all died. The disease did not discriminate between age or youth, strength or weakness, but was savage in its pursuit.

"Two white men came to the camp one day They said that they had traveled many days from far to the south. They came to our camp to ask permission to hunt beaver on our lands. They gave the chief a blanket as a gift, which he handed around for everyone to see. Permission to hunt was given, and they then left.

"Twelve days later the chief awoke, said he felt as if his face and body were burning from the inside, and that his head would burst open with pain. He could barely stand due to the pain in his back. He then collapsed, and threw up blood. Blood also ran from his nose and ears. And then he was dead.

"In the afternoon his two wives died in the same manner. No one could understand why. That night every man who had met and smoked with the white men in the chief's lodge died. Many of the wives and children of these men also died. Some broke out in the spots, as you see on my face and hands, two or three days before death.

"At first the herb doctors gave potions for the sick to drink, in an attempt to stop the burning from the inside. This did no good. Then the herb doctors themselves began to die. After that the medicine man, who had been given great power from the spirits, purified himself in a sweat bath, prayed, tapped his drum, and sang all night long, trying to remove this great evil from our people. He too died the next day."

Stands Alone had great pity for Buffalo Calf. He could see the man was burning with fever, and brought him a ladle of cold water. He also offered some pemmican – a mixture of dried, roasted buffalo meat and ripe sweet chokecherries – which was refused. Stands Alone took off his red cloth neckerchief, a gift from a friend, wetted it, and gave it to Buffalo Calf to wipe his face. Since the weakened man was barely able to remain in an upright seated position on the ground, someone had brought a backrest and placed it behind him.

Buffalo Calf lay against the backrest and took the water gratefully. His throat was so swollen that he had difficulty swallowing. He sipped the water, then continued with his tale of tragedy.

After the medicine man had died, one of the elders said he knew what it was that was killing everyone. His father had told him of a disease that had caused the death of many Nakota near Lake Winnipeg, far to the north. It was brought to them by a member of their band who had visited one of the trading posts of the Hudson's Bay Company. It was called smallpox.

This news had spread through Buffalo Calf's camp rapidly, and panic overcame the village. Cooler heads tried to bring reason back to the normally well-ordered society. But they could not make themselves heard over the screaming mothers, crying babies, and shouts of children and men.

Mothers threw their babies on their backs and ran in all directions. Mothers whose babies had contracted the disease carried them in their arms, only to have the infants die within a few hundred paces of the camp. In some cases, a mother would not realize that her child had died and continued to carry it until she herself collapsed and died. Some of the pregnant women appeared to bleed beneath their skin. Others felt that they were aborting their baby, but died of hemorrhaging through the birth canal.

Unmarried warriors jumped on their war horses and raced away from the camp. Many died in the stampede to leave the village. One girl, about twelve years of age, dashed from behind her lodge and was trampled to death by a running horse ridden by her sister. A grandmother with her grandson in his cradleboard ran out of a lodge, tripped, and fell. The baby lay beside her as the people rushed to leave the camp. His mother rescued him an instant before the grandmother was trampled by a riderless horse. It made little difference. The baby died two days later.

Families scattered in every direction. Few took any belongings except the clothes on their backs. They tried to escape by fleeing, but the evil followed them. They died like buffalo being driven over a cliff. Whole families perished.

The ones who seemed to suffer most were the old men and women. The elderly had difficulty traveling, even under good conditions. Most had been seized by the instinct to flee, but could not because of their infirmities. Knowing this, they resolved to die in their lodges. Over the noises of the confusion, a sharp ear could hear death songs coming from many lodges. Some, when they came down with the fever, took a sharp knife and slit their wrists, or stabbed themselves in the heart.

Five days after the chief and his wives died, Buffalo Calf and his family fled the camp. They had planned to go south, to join this camp near the Little Rocky Mountains, where he now lay dying on the ground. He had hoped that they would escape the disease, because he had been out with a hunting party the day the others sat in the chief's lodge, smoking and talking with the white men.

As they had traveled towards the Little Rocky Mountains, he, his wife Old Hand, and daughter Walking Stone seemed fine. They journeyed until darkness set in, then made camp in a grove of cottonwood trees, near a stream. They tried to eat some of the pemmican from a bag brought by his wife. No one was hungry, and young Walking Stone complained that she had a pain in her head. The parents attributed this to the long day of travel. They had left their camp in such a hurry that all they had with them were the clothes that they wore. They lay on the ground to sleep.

Exhausted after the long day's journey, his wife and daughter fell asleep almost immediately. But Buffalo Calf could not sleep. His mind was troubled by all that he had seen in the last few days: the suffering, the deaths of his friends and relatives. Were others still dying? How many would perish? Would anyone escape this evil? Were he and his two loved ones now out of danger?

Or would the disease, like a terrible black spirit, catch them also? He had no answers to these questions, and his mind was in a turmoil.

He heard a whimper from eleven-year-old Walking Stone, sleeping beside him. To reassure her that all was well, he reached over and gently stroked her brow. She was burning up. In that instant, he knew the answer to his questions.

He picked her up and nestled her in his arms. He felt the burning of her flesh. With tears in his eyes he prayed with desperate fervor, "Wahkonda, ruler of the moon and stars, whose spirit I see in the sun, and hear in thunder, why must my daughter die? Why have not the spirits, which you have given me through my visions, helped me protect my child? The medicine bag hanging from my belt contains everything told to me in the vision of your spirits. Everything that was commanded, I have done.

"I was promised good hunting, success in battle, love, and a good family. Now my first-born, the one I cherish with all my heart, is dying. Why, Wahkonda?"

He held Walking Stone in his arms and rocked her. Even by the faint starlight, he could see the spots that had formed on her face and arms. He continued to rock and sing lullabies to his daughter until the early hours of the morning.

Buffalo Calf had dozed off, but awoke just after the morning star appeared in the east. He caressed the cheek of his daughter and smiled at her. Then he realized that she was no longer breathing. He could not believe his eyes. He put his fingers to her neck, but felt no heartbeat.

She was dead! His body convulsed, and he roared out in a sound of pain and grief. "Why, Wahkonda? Why my beautiful child?"

The sudden shouting startled the sleeping Old Hand, and she bolted upright. "My husband, what ...?" Then she saw the dead child in his arms.

She screamed, "My baby, my baby! Why you, my beautiful baby?" With tears streaming down her face, she laid her head on Walking Stone's breast, and sobbed.

After the sun had risen the sobbing stopped, and Old Hand looked up at her husband. His eyes were red from weeping. She asked, "Husband, what will we do with our daughter now?"

He stared at her for a moment, then replied, "We will put her high in one of the cottonwood trees."

"But what will we wrap her in? We have nothing except our clothes."

Buffalo Calf looked at his child, then at his wife, and said, "We will use my jacket."

With her eyes on the child, Old Hand said, "But your jacket is not big enough to protect her, husband. We will also use my coat. With both she will be safe from the birds and rain until we can come back with a thick hide in which to wrap her."

"But you may need your –"

She cut him off. "Do not worry. The weather is fine, and we will be at our destination in two days. I will be fine."

With loving hands they tenderly wrapped Walking Stone in the two garments and secured them with leather thongs. While Old Hand sat beside the dead child, Buffalo Calf with his long knife cut five lengths of willows about the size of his wrist. These were lashed together with other thin, flexible branches to form a platform. He then climbed high into one of the cottonwood trees and lashed the platform between two sturdy branches.

He climbed down from the tree and returned to where his wife was caressing the bundle. He picked up his daughter and carried her to the base of the tree. There, with the rawhide rope he always carried, he fashioned a sling around her body. With one end of the rope in his hand, he climbed back up to the platform. Old Hand had picked up the body and was hugging it. Buffalo Calf gently lifted the body from his grieving wife's arms and raised it to the platform. There, he placed the body of his daughter with her feet pointing to the west, and lashed it to the platform with leather thongs.

Buffalo Calf climbed down from the tree, took his wife by the hand, and led her away gently. "We must leave now. But will come back soon and take care of Walking Stone properly." They then gathered the horses and continued their journey, leading the horse Walking Stone had ridden.

By mid-morning, Old Hand complained of stomach pains. She said it probably was from not eating since yesterday. She tried to eat some of the pemmican, but could not. A little later she said, "I have great pain in my back. It must be that I am not used to riding these long distances."

Buffalo Calf called a halt to let the horses rest for a short time.

They sat on the ground, and he took his wife's hand. It felt hot, and he knew that she too had been struck by the evil. Looking at her face, he could see the dreaded spots beginning to form.

Old Hand looked back at her husband and could see in his eyes that he knew what she had suspected. She had the disease and would also soon die. The couple, now married for fifteen years, gazed at each other with despair.

Buffalo Calf put his arms around Old Hand, hugged her, and kissed her burning brow.

He said, "Love of my heart, I know of a stream only a short distance to the south. Let us ride a little further. There we can camp, and you can bathe in the cool waters which may stop the burning in your body."

They reached the cottonwood-lined stream about midday. Buffalo Calf lifted Old Hand down from the horse, then carried her to a grassy place near the stream. There he gently laid her on the soft grass, and removed her dress and moccasins. He could see the dreaded spots beginning to appear all over her body.

Old Hand complained of the cold when her fever-ridden body first touched the water. But soon the water felt soothing, and it seemed that the fever had gone down. She felt revived.

In the meantime, Buffalo Calf with his hunting knife cut enough of the soft grass to make a bed for his wife. He then watered and picketed the horses. Returning to his wife, who was still in the water, he said, "Let us camp here. By tomorrow you will be better, and we can continue our journey." Although he knew this was wishful thinking, he meant to raise her spirits.

During the night he felt the brow of his sleeping wife. Her fever seemed to have gone down, giving him hope she would recover. By dawn, however, he again felt her brow and realized that she was dead. By now his emotions had been so dulled by all that had happened that no tears came. He only felt a dull ache in his heart.

With nothing in which to wrap his beloved wife, he could not lash her in one of the trees. With a broken branch, he dug a shallow pit near a fallen cottonwood tree, placed grass in the bottom, and laid Old Hand in the grave. He looked at the ugly spots covering her, but could see only the beauty of the face he had loved. He said, "Goodbye, love of my life." Covering the body, he vowed to come back later to take proper care of her.

That had been two days ago. Since then he had ridden hard. Yesterday, Buffalo Calf realized that he too had been attacked by the evil, but he felt that he must continue so others could be warned of the danger.

The voice of Buffalo Calf was becoming weaker, and more hoarse. Stands Alone offered him more water. Buffalo Calf warned again, "Do not come too close, do not touch me. Put down the ladle where I can reach it." He took the water, barely able to lift it to his lips, and sipped a small amount. For a few moments, he appeared refreshed.

Stands Alone asked, "Buffalo Calf, what happened to my family?" There was no reply. Again, in a louder voice, he asked, "Buffalo Calf, was my family alive when you left?"

Through glazed eyes, both of which were draining a thick fluid, Buffalo Calf looked at Stands Alone. In a voice barely audible, he said, "I saw your grandparents, and they are dead."

His voice became weaker, "Your sister, mother, and father are –"

Buffalo Calf grasped his swollen throat, coughed twice, and was dead. Everyone backed away from the body, afraid that the disease might land upon them next.

Since Buffalo Calf was a lifelong friend of his father, Stands Alone felt it was his responsibility to take care of the body. However, he knew that to touch Buffalo Calf or his clothes could be fatal. He asked a friend for an untanned buffalo hide. Carefully he laid the hide, hair side up, next to the body. Then he and his friend, using long poles as levers, lifted and rolled the body onto the hide. They then rolled the hide and body into a bundle. The ends were tied tightly with wet rawhide thongs. When dried, these would shrink, securing the ends of the bundle so nothing could escape.

The two loaded the body onto a horse and tied it down. They mounted their horses, and led the horse with the body down the valley a good distance from the camp. There they made a platform high in a tree, and onto that they lashed the body of Buffalo Calf. He would be mourned later. Stands Alone had more pressing thoughts.

Was his family safe? Did they escape in time?

Or were they ...? His mind would not let him finish the thought. They would be fine.

Stands Alone wanted to leave immediately, but his friend, Big Snow, convinced him to stay the night, since the sun was already low in the west. Tomorrow they would both ride north to discover the truth about his parents and sister.

That night Stands Alone slept fitfully. The story told by

Buffalo Calf and concern for his family kept him tossing and turning all night.

Stands Alone and Big Snow were up before dawn. They took their horses to the stream to drink. After a quick bite to eat, they loaded a minimum of supplies on the horses and left the village.

They hardly noticed the brilliant reds and oranges that streaked the eastern sky in what promised to be a beautiful sunrise. Their thoughts were not of beauty, but of the death which they would encounter in three days' ride northwest.

The two riders followed the valley in which the camp was located, riding in a northerly direction. Meadowlarks filled the morning with melodic tones, and chokecherries were ripening on the bushes near the stream. They climbed out of the valley and a short time later rode over a small pine-covered ridge as the sun came over the horizon. A large prairie-dog town was crossed, and the dogs barked a greeting as the riders passed. The large rodents were out for their morning meal.

By midday they were just south of the Three Buttes. Rising out of the prairie like sentinels, these buttes were a prominent landmark.

The horses were kept at a steady trot, which would not only conserve energy but allow long distances to be covered in a day. Earlier, they had let the horses drink from a stream they had crossed. Now they stopped and picketed their mounts to graze while the riders ate some of the food sent with them by Big Snow's mother.

To the south, the Little Rocky Mountains were hazy blue in the midday sun. A steady breeze from the west felt cool on this very warm day. When they turned their faces to enjoy the breeze they could see the Bear Paw Mountains a short ride away.

As the sun set, they arrived at a stream flowing not far from the Milk River valley. Stands Alone wanted to continue the journey to the river, but Big Snow was convinced that the horses needed a rest. Besides, mosquitoes would be fierce in the valley. This would be a good place to make camp.

The journey resumed at dawn the next day. They continued to the northwest, and by midday they crossed the Milk River. Predictions by Big Snow had been correct: mosquitoes continually assaulted them as they crossed the valley. They rode to the north side of the valley, away from the biting insects, and followed the river upstream the rest of that day. On the third day they reached the camp of death, located near where the Milk River crosses the present-day border between Canada and Montana.

A short time before they reached the camp, they came across the dismembered bones of what had been a human being. Wolves, coyotes, and birds has picked the bones nearly bare. This was the first sign of horrors yet to come. As they came closer to the camp, more remains could be seen.

When the two rode into the camp, they were nearly overcome by the stench of death. Other than birds, and a few dogs roaming about, no life was evident. Stands Alone searched the village for the markings on the lodge of his parents. When he found the lodge, he saw it had been closed. The entrance flap had been fastened from the outside, and smoke flaps were closed, indications that no one was inside.

Stands Alone dismounted, and began to open the entrance flap. From behind, he heard the voice of an old woman say, "Stop. Do not open the lodge, or you will die." Stands Alone turned and saw a woman he recognized as the village midwife. She appeared to be starving.

The woman said, "I recognize you, my grandson.* You are Stands Alone. Your mother, father, and sister are all dead in the lodge. So few remained from the disease, bodies could not be cared for in the proper manner. Those of us left could do no more than seal the lodges with the dead inside." She continued, "No one must enter the sealed lodges until the bodies have wasted away to bones."

The worst fears of Stands Alone were realized, but with all the devastation, he could not weep. He was beyond tears. He offered the woman food and water from his supplies, which she gladly accepted.

When the time came that only skeletons remained, the bones of those in the lodges, as well those who died trying to escape, would be collected and buried. The skulls would be gathered and taken to the Village of the Dead. These would be placed in a circle, each facing the medicine pole in the center. From this pole, *Wah-Kons* (religious articles) would be hung to protect the sacred place. During certain times of the year, people would go and talk to their friends and loved ones, and leave presents for them.

Stands Alone and Big Snow rode through the village. None of the lodges were inhabited. They were either sealed with the dead inside or had been abandoned. The few survivors had moved their lodges and possessions a short distance upriver. Of the sixty lodges (about four hundred people), only ten lodges

. . . .

* This was a term of endearment used by all elders for persons the age of Stands Alone.

remained. Most of the survivors had lost family members to the evil.

After seeing the condition of the people who were still alive, Stands Alone and Big Snow rode north. Within a short time they came across a small herd of buffalo. They picked out a young bull, which they killed and butchered. The meat was hauled back to the village to be shared by the survivors of the epidemic. The two young men then turned their horses south, toward the Little Rocky Mountains, and rode out of the camp of death.

Months later, they would learn that some infected members of this village had fled to other bands. There the disease spread, and viciously attacked and killed hundreds more of the Nakota.

In all, about two thousand of the Assiniboine people, out of a total population estimated at 25,000 to 30,000, died in the epidemic of 1780 that swept through the tribes of the Upper Missouri.

CHAPTER 3

Wind Walker said, "Husband, you look so sad. Are you all right? Is it something about the baby?"

Startled by her voice, Stands Alone said, "I am fine, and The Boy is beautiful. He will be strong, handsome, and a great warrior some day. His ears are much like yours, small and well-formed, and do not stick out like mine."

She smiled at him, and replied, "But you seemed so far away, and I could see the hurt in your eyes."

He put his arm around her, held her closely and said, "I was thinking of what you had said about our parents. I, too, wish they could be here to see the first grandson on both sides of the family. Can you imagine the feast the new grandmothers would have given to announce the birth of our son?"

He continued, "It would have lasted for three days. The grandmothers would have put all their quillwork skills into their finest designs, competing to make the best clothes for him. At the feast, my father would have given away at least two horses to show his generosity and his pride in his grandson. But they are all gone. That is why I was sad."

Wind Walker kissed his forehead.

The next day Blue Knife Woman and Old Fire came to see how she was doing with the new baby. Wind Walker was surprised when they told her that they wanted to be her son's adoptive grandmothers. Since both grandmothers were dead, someone should make a feast to announce his birth. Wind Walker began to protest; it would be too much work. But they would not hear her. She could not refuse, and was proud to have such good friends.

Blue Knife Woman said, "It is especially good to celebrate the coming of a new baby now. We have not had many new babies since the evil disease of five years ago, when so many of our young people died."

Old Fire said, "It will be a wonderful feast. We will have buffalo-berry soup, boiled buffalo tongue, buffalo roasted over the fire, boiled buffalo, chokecherry pemmican, turnips, and dried juneberries. We will celebrate all night."

"I must ask my husband," said Wind Walker, "but I think he will agree."

That afternoon Wind Walker told Stands Alone of the plans. He agreed happily, and said, "I will give away a horse to one of the elders so that he will go throughout the village to announce the birth of our son."

Early in the evening of the day of the feast, Stands Alone took one of his best war horses and gave it to one of the needy elders. This man led the horse throughout the entire encampment of more than eighty lodges, singing praises and giving thanks for the birth of The Boy, son of Stands Alone and Wind Walker.

The feast began in the early evening, and lasted well into the night. The Boy, whose mother had fed him and tucked him into the clean, soft cattail-down in his cradleboard, slept most of the time. He was carried in his cradle in turn by Blue

Knife Woman and Old Fire, and was introduced to everyone in the gathering.

As the baby was being introduced, Wind Walker's joy was tinged with the sadness of not having the grandparents to share this event. She looked at Stands Alone and smiled. Even by firelight, the pride and happiness in his eyes could plainly be seen.

CHAPTER 4

As she scraped bits of fat and the membrane off the fresh buffalo-hide, Blue Knife Woman said, "Wind Walker, it is nearly the middle of *Wahpegiwi*, the Yellow Leaf Moon (September). It was at this time one year ago that your son was born."

Old Fire interrupted, saying, "Yes, and as his adopted grand-mothers, we will have a great celebration and feast for the event."

All three women stopped scraping the hides, which they were preparing for robes. Old Fire, whose face had begun to show her thirty-seven winters, still had a sparkle of youthful enthusiasm in her voice. She was slightly plump, which was evidence that she enjoyed a good feast at any time. She continued, "We will have smoked buffalo-tongue. And buffalo meat roasted, boiled, and on a spit. And roasted ribs, which are my favorite. Also we will have dried roasted buffalo, as well as fresh elk-meat, roasted turnips, dried chokecherries, juneberry tea with mint, bull-berry soup, and –"

"Old Fire, stop!" said Blue Knife Woman, "You are thinking only of food again. We also plan to have much more than food at this celebration."

Old Fire, slightly embarrassed, broke into her sparkling laugh and said, "Yes, yes. You are correct. But the food will be the best part." They all laughed.

Blue Knife Woman, whose beauty had not been dulled by the many years of hard work, was one year older than Old Fire. She replied, "Yes, I know the food is the best part, but we must speak with the camp crier, to give him names of all the people we will invite to the celebration. Also, we must make arrangements with the medicine man to bless and pray for the child."

"We think the celebration should take place within the next several days," Old Fire informed Wind Walker. "With all the people to be invited, it must be held outside. And at this time of year, we could get snow and very cold weather at any time." The three women discussed the details of the celebration as they continued to work on the hides.

That evening as they were eating, Stands Alone and Wind Walker sat for a time and watched as The Boy, with his several new teeth, chewed on a dried roasted piece of buffalo meat. They laughed as they watched the baby chew and suck on the meat. He laughed back at them. Then Wind Walker lifted the baby to her, hugged him, and he giggled. Stands Alone looked at them both and smiled.

Wind Walker said, "Husband, the two adopted grandmothers plan to give our son a birthday celebration six days from now. They will have more than sixty people at the feast. Do you think it would be the right time to have the medicine man give our beautiful son a formal name?"

Stands Alone thought for a moment, then replied, "Beautiful wife, mother of my son, I say yes, it would be a good time. Tomorrow, I will make arrangements with the medicine man." The couple knew that the two adopted grandmothers would go to great lengths for this event, as it was the custom that in a person's lifetime, only the first birthday would be celebrated.

Three days later Stands Alone spoke with the village chief and the chief of the camp soldiers. He told them of the coming celebration, and explained to the chief of soldiers that he wanted to go and kill a young buffalo bull so that there would be fresh meat for the feast.

He knew that, except in winter time, the rules of the tribe normally did not allow an individual to hunt buffalo. Experience had shown that when individuals hunted alone, everyone hunted on different days and times. In such case, the herd which the camp was following would be constantly disturbed and scattered, making it difficult for all to get the meat needed. Therefore, the rule was to hunt as a group, on a day specified by the medicine man and approved by the soldiers. In this manner, the herd was disturbed for a short time only, and everyone in the camp got sufficient meat to last for many days.

Stands Alone outlined his plan. "Big Snow will go with me. We will approach the animals from downwind, so that they cannot smell us. With their weak eyes, we can get very close without being noticed. We will pick the young bull we want, and once we are within about one hundred paces of the herd, we will crawl until we are within about twenty paces from the bull. At that point, I will kill the animal with my rifle.

"Should he not die immediately, Big Snow will finish the kill with his rifle. Very little disturbance will take place in the herd, except that they will move a short distance. We will then butcher the animal and bring the meat back to camp."

The chief of the soldiers and the village chief discussed the proposal for a short time. Permission was given only because a hunt had not been planned by the entire camp. The next hunt would be at least seven days away.

The next morning, just after daybreak, the two hunters left camp. Shortly after sun-up, they found the herd of more than two thousand buffalo near the location given to them by the scouts who were charged with keeping track of the herd's movement. Their hunting plan worked smoothly. A young bull was butchered, and the meat and hide were hauled back to the camp before noon. The following day, the same two hunters went south to the Missouri River, where they killed and brought back to camp a young elk.

The day before the ceremonies, as was the tradition, Stands Alone presented a gift of one horse and three buffalo robes to the medicine man for his services.

At midday on the day of the celebration, the two adopted grandmothers, both in new dresses, went to the lodge of Wind Walker and presented her with a new sleeping bag for The Boy. It was made of soft white buckskin, and was elaborately decorated with multicolored porcupine quills. The very large hood, which could make it slightly cumbersome, had beautiful designs, made almost entirely with the white man's beads.

Wind Walker was pleased, but not surprised. She laughed, accepted the bag, and said, "I knew the two of you were working on something. You have been so secretive. It is beautiful. I thank you, and my baby thanks you."

Blue Knife Woman said, "All is ready for the celebration. The people are there, and wait for you and The Boy."

Old Fire broke in saying, "The food is all prepared and it smells wonderful. I can hardly wait to taste the ribs." The others looked at her and smiled.

As was the custom the two grandmothers took turns carrying the baby, in the new sleeping bag, to the celebration. Wind

Walker walked behind. When all of the persons invited to the feast had arrived, they had been seated, women on one side of the fire, men on the other. They were talking and laughing when the three women and child arrived. The medicine man stood up, held out his arms, and the crowd became silent.

While Wind Walker took a seat with the women, the two grandmothers carried the baby to the inner circle. Taking turns carrying him, they paraded The Boy completely around the circle for all to see.

The women in the crowd, as well as many of the men, commented on the beautiful decorations covering The Boy's sleeping bag.

Once they completed the circuit, they stopped in front of the medicine man. The medicine man took a long-stemmed, highly decorated ceremonial pipe from its beaded white buckskin case. He filled it with tobacco and a small amount of sweetgrass. Sweetgrass smoke was the medium through which all spirits could be contacted.

He lit the pipe and offered it to the creator, Wahkonda. He presented it to the four corners of the earth: first toward the east where the sun rises; then toward the south where spirits of departed relatives and friends reside; then west; then north; and finally toward the earth.

The medicine man said, "Great Wahkonda, ruler of the wind, moon, and stars, whose spirit we see in the sun and hear in the thunder, take notice of this child we bring before you today. Make him a great hunter, that he may provide for his family. Make him a great warrior, that he may protect his family and Nakota people. May he have success in love, and father many children. Give him a long successful life, and comfort in his old age.

"We entreat you, and the spirits of our departed loved ones, to take part in this celebration. Have pity for the grandmothers who have provided the feast for the child."

The medicine man then pointed to the child in the arms of Blue Knife Woman. She held the baby up for all to see. The adopted grandmothers removed The Boy from his sleeping bag and carried him completely around the circle, this time pausing to introduce him to all.

When they had completed the circle, the medicine man again held up his arms for silence. He said, "Today, with the blessings of Wahkonda, this child will receive a name worthy of great deeds to come."

He motioned to the grandmothers to bring The Boy to him. He held out his hands and said, "Child of Wahkonda, your name shall be Rides With Broken Leg.

"You are so named because of the great deed done by Buffalo Calf when he rescued your grandfather from death at the hands of Piegans. Your grandfather's leg was broken after his horse had fallen. Buffalo Calf, at risk of his own life, came back and lifted your grandfather onto his own horse. They then rode double, to safety, bringing back many horses to our camp."

He put his hand on the child's head and said, "May the spirits of Wahkonda be with you all of your days, Rides With Broken Leg!" The medicine man sat down, and throughout the crowd words of approval could be heard.

At that point, Rides With Broken Leg began crying. He was given back to his mother, who put him to her breast and he became quiet. Blue Knife Woman and Old Fire, along with several other women, served the food. The feast lasted into the evening, and ended with the elders, both men and women, singing songs of thanksgiving for the child as well praising the adopted grandmothers.

When the sun began to settle below the western horizon, Wind Walker, Stands Alone, and their son went back to the privacy of their lodge.

CHAPTER 5

"I have been invited to meet with the master of the buffalo park and several others." Stands Alone told his wife. "I may be late for our evening meal."

It was the middle of *Cuhotgawi*, the Frost Moon (November). Stands Alone's band was nearly ready to break up into three groups for the winter to follow the buffalo as they moved to the southeast. In the summer, the buffalo stayed in large herds of five hundred to as many as six thousand animals. But to survive the winter, the buffalo split up into smaller herds of about fifty to a few hundred animals. By doing this, they could spread out more easily to obtain better grazing.

The Little Rock Mountain Band now numbered eighty-one lodges, with typically about six to eight persons per lodge. This was up from the sixty lodges left after the devastating small-pox epidemic of six years earlier.

Currently, the entire camp was located on the east side of a small stream bordered by cottonwood trees. The buffalo park was a corral-like trap used by the Nakota and their neighbors to the north, the Cree. This one had been constructed the year before. It lay on the west side of the stream. In this land of prevailing westerly winds, it was imperative that the camp be downwind of the approaching buffalo to prevent the animals from getting any scent of humans. Buffalo had weak eyes, but a strong sense of smell.

After a soldier ushered them into his lodge, Bulls Dry Bones, who was both medicine man and master of the park, invited Stands Alone and Four Bears to sit on robes near the entrance. In the back of the lodge was a buffalo skull, painted red. Upon it a small amount of smoldering sweetgrass had been placed as an offering to the Sacred Buffalo, in exchange for the gift of meat and hides. Two other medicine men were seated next to Bulls Dry Bones. Also present were the chief of the band and the chief of the soldiers.

The buffalo-park master and the other two medicine men had spent the last three days and four nights in the lodge fasting, meditating, singing buffalo songs, and praying to the spirit of the Sacred Buffalo to give them success in the hunt to come.

"Last night, in a dream, it was revealed to me that tomorrow is the day to call in the buffalo," Bulls Dry Bones told them. "At daybreak, several of you will ride out, locate the herd, and begin moving them slowly this way. When they reach the proper distance, Four Bears will ride out to meet and call them into the park." Four Bears was well known for his ability to call the buffalo. He had great medicine and was always able to speak to the spirits of the animals.

Stands Alone and the two soldiers present were among the best hunters in the band and could be trusted to find and move the herd to the point where the buffalo could be called into the park. This must be done with care and patience, to keep the animals calm and prevent the loss of the entire herd by a stampede.

After leaving the lodge of Bulls Dry Bones, Stands Alone

went to survey the nearby corral into which the herd would be led. From the enclosure, the lodge of Bulls Dry Bones could not be seen, though only a few paces away, as it was concealed by trees and brush.

As he walked out of the cottonwood trees through the nearly circular park, his thoughts went back to more than a year ago when the site had been chosen and the corral constructed.

Stands Alone and his friend Big Snow had returned to camp after locating a large herd of buffalo for an early spring hunt. They had been riding east, over a nearly level grass-covered plain, when they came upon a small valley. Cottonwood trees lined the small stream. They had ridden down a steep slope. Near the bottom, the steep slope abruptly was broken by a vertical drop, about the height of a man, the bank having been cut by the stream into the hillside many years ago. At the bottom of the cutbank, the valley floor was nearly level.

The two had watered their horses, and sat for a short period talking and eating some pemmican. Big Snow suggested that this valley would be a good place to construct a buffalo park, and Stands Alone had agreed. After returning to camp they discussed the idea with Bulls Dry Bones, who went back with them to view the site. He had readily agreed, and it was not long before construction began. Since then the site had been used successfully several times.

Now standing at the top of the hill, where the entrance began, Stands Alone looked back down at the park. In the floor of the valley, all the trees around the cutbank had been chopped down with axes and cleared from an area of about seventy-five or eighty paces in diameter. Surrounding that area, posts had then been set into the ground at intervals of about three paces.

The space in between the posts had been filled with logs, rocks, limbs of trees, and brush to make a corral.

The last posts were set to create an opening at the cutbank, about fifteen paces apart, so the cutbank could act as the gate to the corral. As the animals came down the slope, they would be forced to jump down this bank into the park, and would not be able to get out again.

In the very center of the corral, a very tall medicine pole had been placed. A long piece of red cloth, which they had gotten from white traders, was hung from the top as a sacrifice to the wind. As an offering to the buffalo spirits, three buffalo skulls, painted with red ocher and decorated with eagle feathers, had been placed at the pole's bottom.

From the top edge of the cutbank, a fence extended from each side, forming a chute that reached to the top of the hill. These structures were made from dirt, stones, brush, and were nearly the height of a man. From the crest of the hill, the two fence lines, or wings – now about half the height of a man – continued, gradually widening out in a V-shape for more than one thousand paces. The buffalo would be called in between the wings, then driven over the crest of the hill, into the final chute, and down over the cutbank into the corral below.

Stands Alone walked back to his lodge and found Wind Walker making a new set of winter clothes for Rides With Broken Leg, whom they still called The Boy. The Boy, now more than one year old, smiled at the sight of his father and continued playing with one of his mother's old moccasins and chewing on a piece of dried roasted buffalo meat.

Wind Walker said, "Husband, I am glad you have returned. The evening food is prepared and will be served shortly."

In the meantime, Stands Alone picked up The Boy, gave him a hug, held him high above his head, and said, "Look how big my son has grown." The Boy spit out the meat and laughed with delight. Then, Stands Alone told Wind Walker, "Make sure the knives are all sharp. The buffalo will be invited into the park tomorrow. The master of the park was given a dream which showed that many buffalo will be killed, and we will have meat to last many weeks. And skins to last many moons."

Well before dawn the next morning, by the light of the half moon, Stands Alone and the two other men had prepared their horses. They mounted, crossed the stream which already had ice along the edges, and rode in a southwesterly direction. As the sun rose, they could see the Bear Paw Mountains to the south, but no buffalo. They turned due west and rode until the sun had moved about one-fourth of the way to its zenith. Then they turned north. They had not gone far when they spotted the herd of about two hundred.

Stands Alone and the others slowly and carefully circled to the west. At that time of the morning, the wind had not yet risen, and the animals did not get the scent of the men. The riders spread out about two hundred paces apart and kept their horses at a walk.

They rode very close to the herd before they were noticed. A calf was first to get their scent and darted into the herd. The riders continued moving very slowly. A few other animals noticed them and moved into the herd. In a short time the entire herd was moving toward the southeast.

The riders continued at a slow pace to push the herd toward the trap. By the time the sun had reached its high point, a strong breeze was coming from the northwest. When the herd was within about two thousand paces of the wings of the park, Stands Alone could see Four Bears waiting in the distance.

Covered with a buffalo robe, Four Bears lay down on the back of his horse and moved slowly toward the herd. He was downwind, so the animals did not get his scent. He rode to within about two hundred paces of the herd before the leaders saw him. At that point, Four Bears made the bleating sound of a buffalo calf. The leaders pricked up their ears. He repeated the sound, and the entire herd began moving toward him. He continued the plaintive cry of the calf and turned his horse toward the wings. The animals followed him.

When he reached the wings of the park, Four Bears nudged his horse into a slow trot, and the herd stayed with him. Increasing his speed, he again called to the animals with the bleating sound. As he moved into the wings, the buffalo began to run after him.

Unknown to the animals, behind the fence-like wings of the trap, humans were hidden. As the last of the herd passed by, a man jumped from behind the barrier and waved a buffalo robe. As the herd passed, other men jumped from behind the barrier waving skins. This continued for the full length of the wings, driving the animals toward the entrance of the chute, hidden over the crest of the hill. By now the entire herd was running at full speed.

In the lead, just before reaching the crest of the hill, Four Bears turned his horse and was immediately outside the wings.

The large bull leading the herd plunged over the crest and down the slope leading to the park below. He saw the trap and tried to stop, but the panicking animals behind pushed him forward. At a full run, he tumbled over the cutbank and fell to his death, his neck snapped. As the herd ran down the hill between the restraining side walls and jumped down into the park through the narrow entrance, more animals fell on top of them and were instantly trampled by others following. It was only a matter of moments before the entire herd had run headlong into the buffalo park.

When Stands Alone topped the hill, he saw a mass of confused animals milling around the corral, bulls snorting and calves bawling for their mothers. Several men sealed the entrance by piling logs and brush between the gate posts of the park. Nearly everyone from the nearby camp, including women and children, surrounded the park.

Even before the gate had been completely closed, the men surrounded the park and began firing arrows, while bystanders shouted encouragement. Though many owned guns, for safety only bows and arrows were used because of the large number of persons around the enclosure. The sun had not gone far beyond its highest point when all the buffalo had been killed.

The master of the park, Bulls Dry Bones, and his two assistants moved through the dead animals to the medicine pole in the center of the park. Here, he held out the long-stemmed lighted pipe, filled with tobacco and sweetgrass, beginning in the direction of the sunrise, then to the south, west, and north, to the earth, and finally to all the animals surrounding him.

Bulls Dry Bones said, "Sacred Buffalo, servant of Wahkonda, the creator of all, we give you thanks for the meat and skins you give us today. You have, as Wahkonda intended, given up your life for the use of our people. Do not feel that you have died for nothing. You have fulfilled your life's purpose by providing for man." He then gave the pipe to one of his assistants, took a piece of braided sweetgrass, and walking among the silent herd, touched each buffalo on the neck.

Only the sound of the wind could be heard until the master touched the last animal. As he moved away, a great swell of talking, laughing, and shouting began immediately. There would be plenty of fresh meat and hides for the entire band. As was the custom, the riders who brought in the herd picked and marked the animals they wanted.

At that point, butchering began and lasted the remainder of the day and all the next day. The work was not finished until late in the afternoon of the third day. Men, women, and children all worked side by side to complete the task.

With The Boy on her back, Wind Walker talked and worked with Blue Knife Woman and Old Fire. Old Fire laughed. "Look how fat the buffalo are," she said. "Tonight we will have a great feast. I can hardly wait to bite into these ribs. And tonight we will have liver, which my husband will want. It is good to have fresh meat again."

The others agreed, and they all worked tirelessly. After partially skinning the animals, the meat was removed from the bones and laid on the hide. The internal organs were also removed and put aside to later be cleansed in the creek. The tongues and hearts were delivered to the ceremonial lodge of the master of the park, to be distributed later to any who requested them.

Every night during the three days of butchering, feasting and visiting took place throughout the camp. Once the butchering was completed, a public celebration would take place, with songs of praise and thanksgiving to the Sacred Buffalo, with speeches, feasting, and social dancing. This celebration would continue for several days.

After the meat was removed, the carcass of each animal was loaded onto a dried buffalo skin and dragged downwind from the camp to be left for wolves, coyotes, magpies, hawks, eagles, crows, and any other scavengers. After the carcasses were hauled away, fresh soil was hauled from the streambank on skins, to cover the ground and remove any sign or smell of the kill.

For the next several days, the women prepared most of the meat for drying. With a sharp knife, a thin cut was made the length of a large piece of meat. The cut was continued around the meat, essentially unrolling it, similar to the way an apple is peeled. Through this process, wide, long, thin pieces of meat were obtained.

These were then hung over poles and turned each day until dry. Then the meat was stored for future use in large rawhide bags. Dried meat was often served boiled or roasted, or could be eaten uncooked. It could also be roasted and then pounded with a stone into nearly a powder form, to be mixed with berries. A small amount of rendered tallow was added to hold it together. This was called *winjascub* by the Nakota, pemmican by the white man.

Once they had taken care of the meat, the women went to work on the hides. They removed the fat and membranes, then hung the hides over poles to dry. When time permitted, the hides would be tanned. At this time of the year the buffalo had grown their winter hair, and most of these skins would be used for robes. The calves' skins were light, even when tanned without removing the hair, and would be used for children's bedding.

As evening approached, Old Fire declared, "I am hungry.

Let us stop this work. It can wait for tomorrow."

She stood up and stretched her back. "I want to go home and have a bunch of roasted ribs. Then we can all go to the celebration and dance."

CHAPTER 6

In her youthful tone, Old Fire said, "These cherries taste so good. I can hardly wait to mix them with a little grease and the dried roasted buffalo meat. They will be even better."

It was *Capasapsaba*, Black Cherries Moon (August). Wind Walker, Old Fire, and Blue Knife Woman had been picking the juicy sweet fruit since early morning. They were some distance from camp, near the northern edge of the Missouri River valley. Wind Walker had left The Boy, now nearly four, with friends at the camp.

At one point, they had seen a grizzly bear not far away, eating cherries in a patch of bushes which looked especially inviting. They yelled at him, trying to scare him away, but all the bear did was grunt several times and otherwise ignore the humans. They decided to try another area.

The entire band of the Little Rock Mountain People was camped on the north side of the Missouri, a short distance upstream from the mouth of the Yellowstone River. Still recovering from the devastating smallpox epidemic, the band was now at ninety-five lodges. Five days ago a very successful buffalo hunt had been staged. Many animals had been slaughtered, and the meat was now drying on poles in the sun. The feasting and celebration of the kill was still in progress during the evenings.

Old Fire said, "We should have thrown stones at the bear, and he would have gone away. Those cherries where he was eating looked extra sweet. If I had had my husband's gun, I would have shot it. Then we could have had the cherries as well as bear meat and grease. I would like a bearskin for the winter."

Blue Knife Woman said, "If we had thrown stones, the bear would have chased us. Besides, you do not know how to load a gun."

"Yes, I do know how," replied Old Fire. "I watched my husband do it many times." She smiled, her lips and teeth stained purple from cherry juice. "Not only do I know how to load ..." She stopped in midsentence and pointed toward the camp. "Look at all the crowd near the river. What could have happened? I hope no one has drowned." The women quickly gathered up the buckskin bags of cherries and started back.

As they approached the camp, they could see that the crowd had surrounded several white men. Most in the band had seen white men only once or twice in their lives, so they were still a novelty.

Wind Walker said, "I wonder if these are the same white men that came to visit us several summers ago."

When the three women reached the crowd, Old Fire said, "Yes, yes, I recognize one of them – the boy we called Young Curly." The name had been given to him when he had visited the Nakota some years earlier, then as a young boy accompanying his father, Big Curly, a trader of goods with the Mandans and other Indian tribes of the Upper Missouri.

Big Curly had seemed interested in opening a trading relationship with the Nakota, who at that time got most of their goods like guns, axes, and kettles in trade from their allies to the north, the Cree, who in turn got the items from the posts of the Hudson's Bay Company. Big Curly had been treated politely, welcomed with Nakota hospitality. In particular, the women in the band had doted on the trader's son, a young lad with golden-brown ringlets of hair. The boy had seldom left his father's side, taking in all the proceedings with his large, blue eyes.

Many summers had passed. And now the son, Young Curly, had returned for a visit to the Little Rock Mountain Band, in the company of several French traders and trappers.

"He is older," Old Fire continued, "but I recognize his curly hair. I wish I had a daughter that I could give to him for marriage. Or if I were younger, I would marry him myself. I know he would have plenty of good food." All three laughed.

The friendly crowd that gathered around the visitors was more curious than anything. Children could be heard talking about the strange clothes worn by the whites. Small groups of women stood watching the visitors as they came into the camp, discussing the hair that covered their faces. Young Curly, as the only clean-shaven one, was also a topic of conversation. Why did he not have hair on his face? What did he do to make his hair so curly?

Several of the band were acquainted with the French trappers and traders among the visitors, men who spoke the Nakota language and with whom the Nakota had done business in the past. Fewer recognized the young American man as the child who had visited the camp years earlier. The white men were taken to the lodge of the chief. Stands Alone and all other council members were invited to sit with the visitors.

The chief welcomed the white men and introduced them to others sitting around the circle of welcoming faces in the lodge. The man sitting on the right of the chief whispered something to him. The chief looked more closely at one of the white men and with a smile said, "You are correct, it is Young Curly. Welcome, Young Curly." He inquired about the father of the young man and was told through the French interpreter that the father had died one year ago. The lodge was quiet for a short time as heads were bowed.

The chief then took the long-stemmed pipe from its case and filled it with tobacco and a small amount of sweetgrass. He lit the pipe and offered it to the four points of the compass, then to the earth. He smoked, then passed it around the circle. Once these ceremonies were concluded, the chief asked the purpose of the visit.

Through the interpreter, Young Curly explained his desire to expand trade with the Nakota, as his father had hoped to do. He presented a new gun, several pounds of gunpowder, a knife, and a bolt of red cloth to the chief as a token of things to come. The chief was pleased, but explained politely that the Nakota desired little that the whites could provide beyond guns, knives, axes, and some iron cooking utensils. Most of these items lasted a long time and would seldom need replacing. Besides, the camp moved often, and possessing too many new things would be an extra burden.

However, he agreed that cloth would be nice for use by the women, although it would never be as strong or as durable as the animal skins which they used.

That night and the three nights which followed, the visitors joined in the celebration and feasting of the successful buffalo hunt. The children were fascinated with the hair of Young Curly. One small child in particular was especially curious and friendly. One evening, the four-year-old Nakota boy brought to the party a small piece of tanned fur. Shyly, he walked up to Young Curly and with great ceremony, presented the fox skin to him.

Young Curly, seated, rose to bow in appreciation. Then he sat down again cross-legged and invited the small Nakota boy to sit down with him, which the child did eagerly, jumping right into Young Curly's lap. In amazement, the child ran his hands through the curly hair over and over, and everyone laughed.

Young Curly asked the child's name, and was told that it was Rides With Broken Leg, known to many as The Boy.

Stands Alone smiled as he watched his son play with the young American trader. But to himself, he wondered about the future. The number of whites coming into their territory was on the increase. They seemed so eager to trade with the Nakota for the skins of the fur-bearing animals, whose winter coats were so long and luxurious. Stands Alone wondered to himself, how would this effect the future of his son – and the Nakota nation?

The whites were offering especially to supply more guns. Would this be something the Nakota needed? It would make hunting easier. But then they would have to buy bullets and gunpowder, as well as the rifles.

At the same time, more guns were being traded to other tribes nearby, some of which were enemies of his people.

And the whites had brought diseases in the past. Could they again bring the dreaded evil that had killed hundreds of Nakota only a few years ago, including his parents? But these white men looked friendly and in good health, and there had been no recent outbreaks of the disease that covered his people with red spots and destroyed their lives in painful agony. But the attack of the deadly illness not long ago had saddened the hearts of the families of the Little Rock Mountain Band so terribly.

Rides With Broken Leg stopped playing and looked up at Young Curly. The white men would be leaving tomorrow, but they would be back. Along with guns, knives, axes, and cloth, they were bound to bring change to the Nakota.

For his son's sake, Stands Alone hoped that change would be good.

CHAPTER 7

"I won! I won again! I can hardly believe it. That makes three times in a row that I have won, and I get to play again," shouted Old Fire above the cheers and laughter of the other women. "I am so glad that men are not allowed in the lodge during the game. Just hearing us from outside the lodge, they must think we are crazy."

She looked around. "Who will be next to challenge me?" Old Fire picked up all of the forty-one sticks used in playing the game. She waved them above her head. "Come, please. Who will be my next victim?" She had made the sticks, which were about the length of her arm from the elbow to the hand, from very thin peeled willow branches.

"I challenge you, and I will beat you," said Blue Knife Woman as she sat down facing Old Fire. "I am so sure of winning, I will wager this," she said, holding up a beaded bracelet, "against that comb you have in your hair."

"It will be your loss," laughed Old Fire. She held all the sticks out in front of her, then slowly lifted and swirled them above her head. With a quick movement, the sticks disappeared behind her back. Her body rocked back and forth as she separated the sticks, all the while staring into the eyes of her opponent. Another swift movement and the sticks reappeared, some in each hand held high above her head. Old Fire slowly brought her hands down, crossed them and held the sticks out to Blue Knife Woman and said, "Pick."

Blue Knife Woman slowly started to reach for the right hand, then changed her mind. She stared intently at the sticks in both hands. "You are not allowed to count, just pick," said Old Fire, shaking her hands. Blue Knife Woman chose the sticks in the right hand of Old Fire, who released them. They both began immediately to count their sticks. "I won, I won again!" shouted Old Fire. "That is the fourth time in a row."

"Are you sure you counted correctly?" asked Blue Knife Woman.

"Yes. Count your own sticks, and you will find that you have an odd number, and you lose. I have sixteen sticks, and I win. You may have more sticks, but I win because I have an even number." Laughing, Old Fire said, "Oh, this Odd Stick game is my favorite. Who will be next to challenge me?"

Blue Knife Woman took off the beaded bracelet and handed it to Old Fire, saying, "We have been playing since before sundown and it is getting late. I have much food prepared. Let us eat before continuing the game."

"Thank you," said Old Fire as she put on the bracelet. "Now, who will be next – oh, did you say food? That sounds good. You always make some of my favorites."

At the request of Blue Knife Woman, Wind Walker carried the large pot of buffalo soup into the center of the circle of women. She poured the soup, flavored with wild turnips, from a buffalo-horn ladle into the trade-goods tin cup which each woman had brought. Blue Knife Woman placed a large wooden tray, laden with smoked buffalo tongue and roasted buffalo ribs, in the center of the circle.

"This soup is so tasty. You always add just the right amount of turnips and grease," said Old Fire. "Oh, I see you also cooked my favorite ribs," as she took one from the tray.

As the others were eating, talking, and laughing, Blue Knife Woman sat down next to Wind Walker and asked, "Did something happen to my adopted grandson today? When he came by here this afternoon his cheeks were streaked with tear marks, and his face and clothes were dirty. I called to him, but he just ran toward your lodge."

Rides With Broken Leg, whose name was often shortened to Rides, was now nine years old.

Wind Walker replied, "Yes, he was dirty. He had been fighting. I got angry with him, but also felt sorry for him. I ended up giving him clean clothes and sent him to the stream to bathe."

"What happened?" asked Blue Knife Woman.

Wind Walker smiled. "Here is the way The Boy told the story." (As his mother, she still called him by his baby name.)

We were down by the stream trying to catch frogs. There were about eight of us in all. The frogs were too fast for us, so we began shooting arrows at them. But every time we shot at a frog, he seemed to see the arrow coming and jumped into the water so we could not hit him.

One of the other boys said we should get our mud-sticks, so we could hit them with mud balls.*

. . . .

* The children's mud-sticks were made of a peeled willow branch, about the length of a man's arm, with one end flattened. A ball of mud or clay was put on the flattened end and thrown at a target.

We threw mud balls at the frogs, but after a while no one wanted to play anymore, because we had hit only two frogs, but they both got away.

One of the older boys said we should play war, fighting with mud balls. I told him that I wanted to try to hit more frogs. He said that if I did not play war, everyone would think that I was a girl.

"Then what happened?" asked Blue Knife Woman. Wind Walker continued The Boy's story.

I did not want to play war, but everyone else did, and I did not want to be called a girl so I played with them. We chose sides, then everyone on my side hid behind the trees along the stream. The other boys charged us.

That same older boy came right at my tree. I threw a mud ball and hit him in the mouth. He stopped, turned, and nearly fell. Just as he turned back to charge again, I hit him with another mud ball. He dropped his stick and came at me. I could see that he was very angry.

I began to run, but he caught up and knocked me down, and hit me in the stomach, and sat on me. I tried to push him off, but he was too big. He took the mud that I had for mud balls and rubbed it on my face and clothes.

Then he said that since I was a little boy, and did not want to play the game in the first place, I should go back to my mother.

Wind Walker finished, "So I gave him a hug and something to eat, and he was better."

Blue Knife Woman said, "That other boy should be punished by his parents. Who was he? As The Boy's grandmother, I will talk to that boy's mother."

Wind Walker replied, "I do not know. The Boy would not tell me."

At that point Old Fire said, "Now that we have finished that delicious food, who wants to be next to be beaten by the Odd Stick champion?"

CHAPTER 8

Rides With Broken Leg awoke with a start and sat bolt upright. He threw off the buffalo robe and, in his night clothes, walked out of the lodge, not even feeling the cold wind coming from the north. The Nakota believed that persons and things seen in a dream were reality, and what he had experienced in his dream was still spinning in his mind.

It was dark and as he wandered through the camp, he nearly fell over a sleeping dog, which barked and ran off whining. He half-heard someone call out to be quiet.

Rides walked back to his lodge, but knew he would not be able to go back to sleep. He must talk to someone about the dream. He now realized he was shivering. It was *Tabehatawi*, Frog's Moon (April), and was still quite cold at night. He would put on a coat and walk more to think about the meaning of the dream. As he prepared to again leave the lodge, his mother whispered, "Son, where are you going? It is not daylight yet."

In a whisper he replied, "I could not sleep, and will take a walk. I will be back after the sun comes up."

After the morning meal, Rides told his parents of the dream. They did not know what it meant, and his father suggested that Rides speak with the medicine man. He would be able to interpret the dream.

About mid-morning Rides went to the lodge of Bulls Dry Bones and asked to speak to him. As he stepped through the opening, the medicine man looked at him and said, "Good morning, my grandson. Come and sit by me. Are you ill?"

Now almost seventeen years old, Rides replied, "Thank you, grandfather. I am not ill, but last night a strange thing happened while I was sleeping." He paused, remembering the vivid dream. "It was so clear, I could smell the smoke of sweetgrass. Then I realized I was sitting on a beautiful black horse. From above came the sound of wings. I looked up, but could see nothing except a few white clouds. A voice, which came from the location of the sound, said, 'Look in the distance, my son.' I looked and saw a large herd of buffalo. The voice then said, 'Look down, my son.' I looked down and saw a warrior, not of the Nakota, lying face down on the ground."

He looked up, startled, as if just returning again from the world of the dream. "Then I was awake in my lodge. Can you tell me what it means, grandfather?"

Bulls Dry Bones sat for a few moments with a distant look in his eyes, then said, "You are very fortunate, my grandson. One of the spirits of the Thunderbird has taken favor with you. It was that spirit which spoke to you."

"But grandfather, what does it mean – the smoke, the horse, the buffalo, the man on the ground?"

"It seems very clear, my grandson. The sweetgrass smoke is sacred to both the spirits and the Nakota. This tells us that it was a true spirit of the Thunderbird. The spirit was telling you of future success in stealing many horses from other tribes. The herd of buffalo meant that you will always have plenty of meat and robes for your family. The man on the ground was a sign that you will be a great warrior, and some day count many coups."

"Grandfather, how do I contact this spirit?"

"My grandson, do not worry. I will make a medicine bundle which you can use to contact your guardian spirit. It will contain all the symbols the spirit gave to you. Sacred sweetgrass, dried buffalo meat, mane from a horse, human hair, and an offering of tobacco. You must never tell anyone what the medicine bundle contains, or it will not work. When you pray to your spirit, call for him by the name 'Sound Of Wings.' I believe that it would make your spirit happy for you to pledge to dance in the next sacred Medicine Lodge Dance."

The Medicine Lodge Dance (later known as the Sun Dance), was the major religious and social event of the year for the Nakota. Preparations had begun not long after the last snow had melted, when the first thunder could be heard.

Bulls Dry Bones, the medicine man, had inherited the gift of making a Medicine Lodge Dance from his grandfather. He collected the offerings to the Thunderbird, which was embodied in the lightning and thunder. It was the invisible symbol of Wahkonda, the Universal Power, whose home was said to be in the sun.

The Medicine Lodge Dance was hosted by a single band or several bands together. The ceremony was held in thanksgiving for aid granted, and new petitions were made to the Thunderbird and all its spirits.

The rules and regulations of making a Medicine Lodge Dance were very strict and had to be followed closely, if communications were to take place between humans and the spirits of the Thunderbird. If the ceremonies were followed correctly, the Thunderbird and its spirits would be obligated to grant the Nakota success in hunting and war, along with health, plentiful food, and the well-being of the band or entire tribe.

Early in *Wedu* (spring), Bulls Dry Bones had called the head-men to the ceremonial lodge. In the back of the lodge, a sacred fire of braided sweetgrass was burning. The medicine man presented the offering of tobacco, scarlet cloth, and a choice piece of buffalo meat to the spirit. He sang ceremonial songs, and prayed while one of the men hung the cloth from the lodge poles near the sweetgrass. Bulls Dry Bones then put the meat offering into the fire while continuing to pray that the ceremony would be acceptable to the spirit. At last a small hole was dug in the center of the lodge, and the tobacco was buried as an offering to the earth.

Two similar ceremonial meetings were held during the next two moons. During this period, the camp moved several times to keep up with the buffalo, which after the winter were again gathering in large herds. The Little Rock Mountain Band, now located about one day's ride northeast of the Little Rocky Mountains near the Milk River, was joined by the Missouri River Dog Band. The circular camp contained more than two hundred lodges.

It was the middle of *Waheqosmewi*, Full Leaf Moon (June), when Bulls Dry Bones and two assistants camped a short distance from the main village near the Medicine Wheel. The Medicine Wheel had been constructed by Nakota medicine men many years earlier. Stones from far to the north, carried into the area by glaciers and deposited thousands of years ago, were used to construct the wheel. It had been laid out on the ground, about twenty paces in diameter, with spokes representing the great wheel of the sun and stars and their special alignments throughout the year.

The three men were especially interested in the spoke that represented the summer solstice. At dawn on that day – midsummer – the sun would be in direct alignment with that particular line of stones. When midsummer day came, Bulls Dry Bones calculated the number of days until the next full moon. At that time, the Medicine Lodge Dance would begin. It would last two nights and one and one-half days, during which time the participants would not eat or sleep.

The fourth and final ceremonial meeting took place the night before the dance began. The singing, led by Bulls Dry Bones and the master of ceremonies, continued until dawn. The master of ceremonies was the first man to pledge to participate in the Medicine Lodge Dance to fulfill a commitment. It was held in a lodge specially constructed for this purpose. Along with the drummers and singers were all those who had pledged to participate in the dance. Rides With Broken Leg had pledged to join the ceremony after Bulls Dry Bones had interpreted his dream.

The master of ceremonies made a prayer to the earth and the sky. Bulls Dry Bones then buried an offering of tobacco near the center of the lodge. Again, a sacred fire of sweetgrass burned in the rear of the lodge, above which scarlet cloths were hung as offerings to the sky spirits. Near the fire, a crescent moon was drawn on the earth.

As the sun began to rise, Bulls Dry Bones said a final prayer to the spirits of the Thunderbird. The master of ceremonies then called the most famous warriors of both bands to come to the center of the camp. They were instructed to scout for a tall straight cottonwood tree, with a high fork, which would become the center pole for the Sacred Medicine Lodge. First, the warriors counted coups, reenacting their brave deeds in the field of battle, then set off as a group to scout for the tree.

Once the tree was selected, the scouts returned, handed a branch to the master of ceremonies, and said that "the enemy" (the tree) had been located.

The warriors then returned to the location of the tree, followed by the entire camp. Rides With Broken Leg had ridden to the site with other young men pledged to join the ceremony.

Upon reaching the selected tree, the medicine man and the master of ceremonies walked four times around the tree, made four small fires of sweetgrass, and tied a scarlet cloth around the trunk. Prayers were offered to the tree, and it was told of the function it would perform. As a symbol of the spirits of the Thunderbird, it was asked to take pity on the people and fulfill the needs and desires of the Nakota.

Once the prayers were finished, the two shook their rattles and sang Medicine Dance songs. They appointed two of the scouts to cut down the tree. The scouts made three passes at the tree and on the fourth, they sunk their axes into the trunk. Moving around the tree in the direction of the sun, using only left-handed strokes, they cut it down

As it began to fall, the remainder of the scouts fired their rifles into the branches and leaves, and scrambled to be the first to touch the leaves and strip a branch off the fallen tree.

With all the branches stripped, short poles were placed beneath the tree, and the scouts, working in pairs, carried the tree back to the camp. On this bright sunny day, the entire camp followed in procession, carrying or dragging additional poles and branches with the leaves intact.

This was a precious time for lovers and sweethearts. It was the only day of the year that the young women were not chaperoned. The women dressed in their finest dresses and rode double with their chosen man. The older women joined in the songs of war begun by the scouts. Some of the young couples half-heartedly joined in, but soon their singing died out. They were more interested in each other.

Old Fire watched the young couples come into the camp. "If our grandson had not pledged, I know many of the young women would want to be riding with him as he is so handsome."

Once the entire procession reached the camp, the center pole was stripped of bark, then carved in zigzag lines to represent lightning. The fork had been left at the top of the pole, and there a nest of branches and leaves was built – the nest of the Thunderbird. A crescent was carved beneath the nest to represent the new moon. At the base of the pole, a buffalo head was carved. The pole was then set up under the direction of Bulls Dry Bones.

Together, the master of ceremonies and the medicine man supervised the construction of the lodge. A framework of poles formed a conical roof, extending from the fork at the top of the center pole outward to a circular structure of posts and crossbars that formed the outer wall of the lodge. This lodge was then partially enclosed by branches and leaves entwined throughout the framework. When finished, the lodge would allow forty dancers or more to participate in the ceremony.

A large opening was left on the south side of the Medicine Lodge for spectators.

Inside the lodge, all around the inner wall, a screen about breast high was constructed of cherry branches and leaves. Behind this screen, in an alley left between the screen and the lodge wall, the participants would dance. In this space, men and women dancers would be separated midway by a curtain made of cherry branches.

After the Medicine Lodge was built, Bulls Dry Bones tied strips of scarlet cloth to the center pole. In the back of the lodge, behind the screen, he made an alter of sagebrush, upon which was placed a buffalo skull.

Evening was approaching by the time the Medicine Lodge was completed. At this time of the year, the sun was still high above the horizon and the sky was still blue. No clouds could be seen, and the air became cooler. The ever-present breeze of the daytime had stopped.

The participants took their places behind the screen. The men singers, with their long drumsticks, sat in the northeastern part of the lodge. Women singers sat to the south of them. Bulls Dry Bones waved a dry buffalo-hide over their heads three times, praying after each wave. When he finished the last prayer, he threw the hide, with a strip of hair left on, down the center. It was a reminder that the Nakota depended upon the buffalo for their existence. The singing began, and the drummers began tapping the dried buffalo-hide.

The men who danced wore only breech-clouts. About their heads, some wore a wreath to represent various spirits, such as the deer or sagegrouse. Rides With Broken Leg wore a wreath made from a strip of tanned buffalo hide, around which was intertwined some hair from the mane of a horse, some human hair, and sweetgrass.

The dancers moved up and down, staying in one place, each blowing an eagle-bone whistle. The peeping of the whistles represented the sound of infant Thunderbirds.

Blue Knife Woman said, "I am glad our adopted grandson is dancing in the Medicine Lodge. He has become so handsome. It seems only yesterday that we had the feast for his first birthday." Wind Walker and Old Fire agreed. The three were in the front row of the crowd watching the dance.

Old Fire said, "After the dance is finished, we must give a feast for our grandson to celebrate his good fortune. Let's see, we will have young sagegrouse, buffalo meat, fresh juneberries, and –"

Blue Knife Woman interrupted with a smile, saying, "You are already thinking of food. But the dancers must fast until the dance is finished. I am happy that at least they can drink water."

By the time the moon had reached its zenith, most of the crowd had gone back to their lodges. The singers had been changed three times, and the dance continued. Rides continued the knee-jerking dancing, up and down, while blowing the eagle-bone whistle. He silently prayed to the Thunderbird and his guardian spirit. The drums, singing, and dancing made him feel euphoric. As he concentrated on his dream, he tried to imagine what his spirit, Sound Of Wings, must look like.

Through the night and the next day the dance continued. The drummers and singers had rotated several times. By the middle of the second night, four of the men and two of the women dancers had collapsed from the rigors of the dancing, and had to be carried to their lodges.

The end of the dance came on the second day, when Bulls Dry Bones held up his arms and announced that the sun had reached its high point. Rides With Broken Leg was nearly exhausted and thanked Sound Of Wings for helping him finish the ceremony.

When the drummers and singers had finished their last song, the medicine man prayed, "Thunderbird – representative of Wahkonda, the creator of the universe – through your spirits, bring us rain so that the grass may grow, so the buffalo will increase and become fat. Bring us prosperity. Do not allow sickness to fall upon the Nakota. Direct your spirits to give us aid in war. Take pity upon us."

Bulls Dry Bones had just completed the prayer and was about to signal the ceremony's end, when he saw a young women carrying a small boy in her arms moving toward him. She said, "Grandfather, please help me. My husband was killed when his horse fell on him, and my son has been very ill and does not get better. I am afraid he is going to die too."

The medicine man looked at the child who appeared to be starving and dehydrated. "What is wrong with the boy?" he asked.

The mother replied, "When he eats or drinks, he throws up the food, or it causes looseness of the bowels." She was distraught, clutching her listless child in her arms.

"Bring the child nearer to the center pole." Bulls Dry Bones then stepped to the sacred center pole. He danced three times around it, and sang a song in a language no one could understand. He then stood in front of the pole, staring intently up at the nest. He appeared to be in a trance. After a short time, he took a length of braided sweetgrass, held it up, then tapped the pole and ran the sweetgrass down the carved zigzag line, praying as he moved.

When the buffalo head inscribed at the base of the pole was reached, Bulls Dry Bones picked up a hollow buffalo-horn and held it to the pole. Water trickled from the pole into the horn.

A murmur of amazement went through the crowd. Bulls Dry Bones turned and held out the horn for the woman. He said, "Take this and give it to the child. Let him drink all that he wants."

The woman, with tears in her eyes, said, "Thank you, grandfather. My son thanks you, and my dead husband thanks you. I will pray to the Thunderbird for you everyday."

The medicine man replied, "Take the boy to your lodge. Let him drink and give him food, and do not worry. He will grow up to be big and strong." He then turned to the dancers and said, "The dance is finished."

That afternoon the Medicine Lodge was taken down. All that remained was the center pole with the offerings left intact. It was believed that anyone who touched the offerings would be struck by lightning. By late afternoon, the entire camp had been moved a short distance upstream along the Milk River. A short time before sunset, a cloud came up in the west.

Out of it came flashes of lightning, and distant thunder could be heard. Bulls Dry Bones stepped out of his lodge and walked to the center of the camp. In his strong voice, he said, "This is a sign – that the offerings, sacrifices, and prayers of the Nakota are acceptable to the Thunderbird. The year to come will be good."

That evening, families held feasts for their relatives who had participated in the dance. Rides' parents and his adopted grandmothers prepared a great feast and invited many friends, including some from the Missouri River Dog Band. As a gesture of thanks and pride, Rides' father, Stands Alone, gave two horses to Bulls Dry Bones – one for interpreting the dream of Rides, the other for the successful dance.

Rides was nearly exhausted, but was enjoying the feast. He was especially happy for the pride seen in the faces of his parents and adopted grandmothers. It was twilight as he watched the moon, which had been full three days ago, rise. As he watched, his thoughts wandered back to the dance – and to his guardian spirit.

He had nearly dozed off when she appeared. In his state of mind, he first thought that it was a vision of his spirit, Sound Of Wings. Then, as his mind focused on the present, he realized it was indeed a beautiful girl, dressed in white buckskin decorated with colored quills. She wore white moccasins with matching leggings, and her long braided hair, which glinted in the moonlight, hung down in front of her.

As she approached, Rides leaped to his feet, his heart pounding. With her chaperone standing behind her, she said with a smile, "You are Rides With Broken Leg. I am Spotted Leg from the Missouri River Dog band. For the last two days, I have watched you dance. You are very strong. You never seemed to tire."

Rides' heart was pounding so hard that all he could manage was a simple thank-you. At the same time he was thinking, she is beautiful. Why haven't I seen her before? What do I say next?

However, he did not have to say anything. Spotted Leg continued, "Tomorrow, after you have rested, please come to my lodge. It is the one painted with a white buffalo and black horse. We can walk about the camp." Still smiling, she turned, and with her chaperone following, strode toward her parents lodge.

All he could do was blurt out another weak thank-you as she left. He again had that feeling of euphoria. Had she been a dream? As he fell asleep that night, the last thing on his mind was the vision in white.

Rides awoke early and had the morning meal with his parents. His mother gave him a potion to take. She said it was from one of the herb doctors, and it would help his sore leg muscles. Rides felt little pain in his legs – until he tried to walk. The two nights and day and a half of dancing had taken its toll. His adopted grandmothers came by and again congratulated him for his part in the dance. Shortly after they left, Rides lay down and did not awake until mid-afternoon.

Wind Walker prepared some dried buffalo meat and juneberries for him when he was fully awake. At that point he told her of the invitation extended to him by Spotted Leg. His mother paused a moment and then replied, "Rides, I am sure that she is a very nice girl. I have met her mother, and she is very pleasant."

That evening after the meal was finished, Rides dressed in his finest clothes and walked to the lodge of Spotted Leg. As he approached the lodge, the vision in white appeared smiling at the entrance. To Rides, she seemed more beautiful than she had last evening. She was again dressed all in white buckskin, but now her braided hair was tied in a knot behind her head. A small amount of red paint colored her cheeks. She seemed to float toward him and said, "Rides With Broken Leg, it is good to see you again. You look much rested since last evening."

His mouth felt dry, but he replied, "Ah, I, ah ... thank you. Wasn't the sky beautiful today, especially after the rain shower we had last night?" Then he blurted out, "You are beautiful."

Casting her eyes down modestly, Spotted Leg said, "Thank you. I think you look very handsome. This is the first time I have seen you fully dressed and not just in the breech-clout worn for Medicine Lodge Dance." And then she laughed.

At that moment her chaperone stepped from the lodge. She walked to the couple and Spotted Leg introduced Rides to her. She was Spotted Leg's grandmother.

"Let us go for a walk," said Spotted Leg, "and grandmother will accompany us." They strolled around the camp, with the grandmother three paces behind, and everyone seemed to notice them. A young man with a beautiful girl – Rides thought that his chest would burst with pride.

As they walked, he asked her about her life, and she in turn asked about his future. When they reached the edge of the camp, the moon was well above the horizon. They stood for a moment, struck by the sight. Rides said, "The moon is beautiful. Like you."

She smiled, reached out, and touched his hand. Just as she did, her chaperone said, "My grandchild, it is time to go back to our lodge."

Just after sunrise the next morning, the Missouri River Dog Band began to break camp. Rides went to the lodge of Spotted Leg, but the lodge had already been taken down. He almost panicked, thinking that he would not see her again. He ran through the nearly empty camp until he found her. Spotted

Leg was riding a black horse which pulled a travois loaded with her family's lodge.

Nearly out of breath when he reached her, he said, "I was afraid I would never see you again."

"I am happy that you came, but I knew that I would see you again, though it were not today." She reached out her hand, which he took. She squeezed hard and said, "Come visit our band one day."

Rides flushed and weakly replied, "Thank you, I will."

Then in the distance he heard her grandmother say, "Come, Spotted Leg. It is time to go."

As he watched, the vision slowly blended in with the rest of the band in the distance.

CHAPTER 9

Rides With Broken Leg froze as the man approached him. He tried to stop breathing, but could not. He was sure his pounding heart could be heard by the Crow warrior who stood staring directly at him in his hiding place. The man's eyes had a yellow glint in the pale moonlight. Then the man turned, and Rides breathed a little easier. The man had come out of his lodge to relieve himself.

It was some time before sunrise, and the waning moon was low in the western sky. As the man turned, the moonlight reflected off his neck; a scar appeared as a long dark line, and the upper part of his left ear was missing. Rides With Broken Leg recognized him as the Crow warrior with whom his father, Stands Alone, had fought a few years ago.

Six winters ago a party of Crows, longtime enemies of the Nakota, had sneaked into the camp of the Little Rock Mountain Band late one night during a full moon to steal horses. They had been discovered, and a running battle had ensued. Stands Alone had lunged at the horse of one of the enemy who was trying to retreat from the camp. He had caught the man's leg and pulled him to the ground. The two then locked in combat with knives.

The Crow had thrust his knife at Stands Alone, who quickly

sidestepped and slashed the enemy's throat. The Crow warrior staggered but had stayed upright as blood spurted from the wound. As the raider turned to flee, Stands Alone again swung his large knife, this time severing the upper part of the man's left ear. Just then several of the retreating Crow had charged past on their horses, with many Nakota in pursuit. In the confusion the Crow warrior had escaped, but it was assumed that he had died of his wounds.

After relieving himself, the Crow with the half ear yawned, glanced at the moon, and turned back toward his lodge. He took three steps, then stopped casually, turned halfway around, and looked directly again at the place where Rides lay hidden. The dark scar stood out in the moonlight. The Crow then walked slowly back and entered his lodge, which stood about one hundred paces from where Rides lay. Rides did not move but continued to watch for further activity among the sixty lodges. Nothing stirred.

When he felt that sufficient time had elapsed for the man again to be asleep, Rides slowly moved to his right where Buffalo Capture was watching the corral of Crow horses. He signaled to Buffalo Capture, and they both moved slowly back to the spot where the other members of the party were hiding.

Plans for this raid on the Crow began five days after the Medicine Lodge Dance. Red Leggings, a well-known Nakota warrior, felt that the time was right to raid one of the Crow villages. But before final planning could be done, he had to get permission from the chief of the band and the chief of the soldiers.

He brought before the two chiefs his plans – to march south about five days, cross the Missouri River to the Yellowstone, locate a Crow village, and steal their horses. After much discussion with the chiefs and their advisors, Red Leggings was given permission to form a raiding party.

Early in the morning the day after the meeting, Red Leggings rode out of the village. A half-day's ride from his village, he reached a small stream where he set up camp. By mid-afternoon he had constructed a sweat lodge, half the height of a man and two paces in diameter, made of willow branches covered with grass and cattail leaves. A hole had been dug in the center of the lodge and was lined with rawhide.

Outside the lodge, a fire was built into which he put several stones. As the stones heated, he hauled water from the creek in a rawhide water bag and poured it into the lined hole inside the lodge. The hot stones were then carried into the lodge with a forked stick and dropped into the water. Once all the stones were in the water, Red Leggings stripped naked, entered, and covered the opening of the lodge from the inside with willows and cattails. Steam completely filled the interior. The man sat meditating as perspiration poured from every part of his body.

Before the sun had set, the man emerged from the sweat lodge with both his mind and body purified. He bathed in the cool water of the stream, then lay down on the grassy bank and let his body dry. He dressed himself in white buckskin pants and shirt, decorated with beads.

His horse, which was tied to a stake, nickered. Red Leggings untied the rope and led the animal to the stream and let him drink. Then he took the horse to a spot a short distance from the sweat lodge. With a long braided rawhide rope, the animal was tethered to a stake. The horse began immediately to graze on the lush grasses along the streamside.

Red Leggings returned to his bag of supplies and removed his ceremonial pipe, tobacco, sweetgrass, and a piece of red cloth. He took the cloth and tobacco to the top of a nearby knoll, where he drove a stick into the ground. To it he tied the cloth. He then buried a small amount of tobacco. These were sacrifices to wolves, the spirits of war. If his sacrifice was accepted, the wolves would howl. If not, these spirits would be silent.

He returned to camp and took out his pipe, putting a mixture of tobacco and sweetgrass into the bowl. Lighting it with an ember from the dying fire, Red Leggings presented the pipe to the four corners of the earth, then to the sky and the earth.

He puffed the pipe and blew the sacred sweetgrass smoke into the air. This was the medium through which he would contact his guardian spirit. From a willow tripod, he took his medicine bag containing items told to him in a dream by his guardian spirit. Holding it, he sat down and prayed, "Spirit, keeper of my life, guide me in making a raid on the Crow enemy. Give a sign of your blessing to show that you will be my strength and protection in the fighting to come. Help me gain many coups." To the east, the evening star had come over the horizon.

For the next two days Red Leggings fasted, meditated, and continued to pray for a sign of good fortune. Not long before the moon rose on the third night, he dozed off. In his sleep, he heard the singing and drums of the Victory Dance in the distance. At the last crash of the drums, he suddenly awoke. He listened further, but heard nothing except the noises of the night.

Red Leggings' heart was pounding. This was surely a sign from his guardian spirit that the planned raid would be successful. He tried to go back to sleep, but could not. He looked into the sky and wondered at the power of Wahkonda. His heart marveled at the beauty of the morning star, soon made invisible by the brilliance of the sunrise. His whole being felt a part of this beauty, and as he fell asleep, he heard the distant howl of a wolf pack.

Two days later Red Leggings gave a feast. To the seven young men sitting in the circle, he said, "This feast is made in your honor. I have had a sign from my spirit and from the wolves that I will be successful in leading a raiding party against the Crow. I have invited each of you for special reasons." He enumerated the reasons for invitations extended to each of the seven. Some were chosen for their shooting ability, some for swiftness in running, and some because they had been on a successful raiding party before. Later in private, Red Leggings would confide to Rides With Broken Leg, "You were the first to be invited – because of your vision and its interpretation by the medicine man."

Each of the young men, aged from thirteen to eighteen years, showed excitement in being chosen for this raid. War was a part of the culture of the Nakota. From early childhood, boys were taught that the way to gain status was to show courage and bravery in war. This brought pride to relatives – and the admiration of young unmarried women. Coups in war also brought invitations to join warrior societies. On the other hand, without status gained in this manner, most societies were closed to them and they would be held in contempt by relatives and eligible young women.

Before the feast was finished, Red Leggings said, "We will begin our journey two days before the moon is full. Bring your favorite weapons, but do not carry too many as we will be walking. Also bring eight pairs of moccasins, as the distance is great." There was no need to tell each to bring his medicine bag and his shield made from the thick skin of a buffalo's neck. Each man's shield was round, with two to three eagle feathers attached to the edge and painted with the signs which the spirit had given to that warrior.

The night before the party was to leave, they all met in the soldiers' lodge where they would spend the night. After they had eaten, all participated in the Crow Dance, sponsored by the War Society. Each participant wore a headdress made from the entire skin of a crow, including the head and wings.

As the sun rose the eight men, their faces painted red, left the village singing songs of the Wolf Society and songs of death. Led by Red Leggings, they walked single-file south through a vast grassland which was broken only now and then by a dry stream or pine ridge. To the west, the Little Rocky Mountains appeared blue in the distance.

By late afternoon, the plain changed abruptly into a seemly endless number of eroded gullies and ravines. They had reached the breaks, or badlands, of the Missouri River. The mighty river had cut this great twisted, tortured gash in the earth's crust thousands of years ago, after being displaced by glaciers to shift nearly one hundred miles south of its original course. The badlands were a natural barrier between the territory of the Nakota and their traditional enemies, the Crow.

Except for occasional clumps, the prairie grass had nearly disappeared. It was replaced by sagebrush, greasewood, and clusters of scrubby pines gathered here and there. The party descended the steep slopes of nearly barren clay soil. The dark gray color of the earth was occasionally flecked with the nearly white fossilized shells of sea animals which had died millions of years ago. Some of the raiding party picked up and kept pieces of the fossils as good-luck charms.

The descent through this steep, highly eroded terrain ended as abruptly as it began. The party rounded a bend in a gully and one by one, walked out onto the nearly flat plain of the Missouri River bottom.

The lack of vegetation during the descent contrasted with the sudden abundance of willows and cottonwood trees near the river, and clumps of juneberry and cherry bushes along the valley edge. All were a welcome sight.

Red Leggings looked about and said, "The sun is getting low. We will camp there," pointing to a stand of willows. Each man unloaded his supplies. Red Leggings gave instructions, "Slow Walker and Iron Man, go look for small game in the vicinity. Buffalo Capture and Red Mane, it is late in the season, but go and see if there are any juneberries left on the bushes. Stone Leg and Long Arrow, gather wood and make a fire. Rides With Broken Leg will help me build a raft."

A short time later a fire was burning. An iron cooking pot filled with water was set by the fire to heat. The berry pickers returned with a bag full of fruit. All four helped lash together the poles which had been cut by Rides and Red Leggings to make a raft. Before the sun set, the two hunters returned with four sagegrouse.

Slow Walker cut up one grouse and put it into the pot to cook, while Iron Man put the other birds on long willow skewers and began roasting them over the fire. By the time the raft was complete, the birds were cooked. Slow Walker removed the meat from the boiling pot and put in four handfuls of juneberries to make a tasty soup which they drank from wooden bowls. Once all had eaten, Red Leggings laid out the plans for the raid.

The sun had long set and the evening star shone brightly, but twilight still played in the western sky as the group made ready for sleep. They would not need a sentry tonight.

Rides With Broken Leg held his medicine bag and prayed to Sound Of Wings, his guardian spirit, "Spirit who chose me, give us success in our raid against the Crow. Protect from harm all that are in our party and help us count many coups." The words hardly escaped his throat when from the rim of the breaks high above came the war spirits' reply: the howl of the great gray prairie wolf.

Shortly after sunrise the next morning, the group crossed the Missouri River. Two trips with the raft were needed to get everyone and their supplies across.

They traveled downstream for a short time to the point where the Musselshell River entered the Missouri. Several times they saw the bouncing flash of a flag-like tail, as white-tailed deer dashed through the woods and brush in the valley bottom. They all laughed as a playful beaver slapped its tail on the water as it floated downstream on the current.

The party turned south and traveled up the Musselshell River valley. In mid-afternoon Red Leggings called a halt. "We are now near Crow territory, so we will rest here until after dark. We will travel by night until we reach our goal. The moon gives enough light so we can travel in safety, and we will be guided by the stars." On the second night, they left the Musselshell valley at the great bend where the river turns west.

The raiders continued south, guided by the North Star.

They slept by day, taking turns at watch. It was now too dangerous to build a fire, so they ate from their supplies of dried meat and pemmican. They continued south for two more nights. By the middle of the following night, they reached the sandstone bluffs guarding the northern side of the Yellowstone River valley. The entire party looked over the bluff to see the waning moonlight reflecting off the tranquil river far below.

Rides With Broken Leg said, "Look to the west. I see lodges." The Crow lodges appeared gray in the glow of the moon.

"There are about sixty lodges," said Red Leggings. "With that number there should be at least one hundred horses. We will stop here. It is not long until we see the first light of day. We will spend the day here and watch the Crow village."

They watched from their vantage point until the light of the new day obliterated the stars and subdued the light of the moon. Red Leggings said, "Let us find a secure place for the day. Early tomorrow morning, when the moon is still bright, we will make our raid and steal all their horses."

They searched and found a large crevice in the massive sandstone bluff with room for twice their number. It would conceal them from any random passersby, yet they could still observe the Crow village. The day was spent resting, eating, and planning the raid and escape route.

"The moon was full three days ago," said Red Leggings. "It rises later each night and sets later each morning, so there will still be plenty of moonlight when we strike halfway between the middle of the night and sunrise." He continued, "Eat well tonight, for you may not eat for the next two days and nights during our escape. All things such as food, extra moccasins, and any items other than weapons will be left here when we leave."

The sun was low in the west when Red Leggings took his war shirt from his supply bag. The shirt, made of smoked buckskin, was decorated in back and front with dyed porcupine quills. His guardian spirit had given the design to him in a dream, and it was later made by his wife. He believed it to be impenetrable by arrows, lances, and bullets.

Shortly after moonrise, the party left the security of the crevice and descended into the Yellowstone valley. They reached the river and followed the northern bank where trees and brush concealed them from the Crow village. They made their way to within about three hundred paces from the village when Red Leggings held up a hand to halt.

He spoke in a whisper as the seven men gathered around him. "Rides With Broken Leg and Buffalo Capture, move closer to the village and watch a while. We need to know if the horses are guarded. If there is a guard, we will need to overpower or kill him. Return when everything is quiet, fires are out, and no one is stirring. Then we will decide how to take their horses."

When the moon was in the west, Rides and Buffalo Capture returned to report what they had seen. Red Leggings asked, "Rides, are you sure that the man you saw was the same one who fought your father many moons ago?"

"He has only one half of his left ear, and I could see what seems to be a long knife scar on the right side of his neck. It was as my father described it. It has to be the same man," said Rides With Broken Leg.

"Then we must be very careful. He is a very strong and cunning warrior. He is afraid of nothing and enjoys killing

Nakota. Two summers ago, he and a group of Crows attacked the Missouri River Dog Band at night. They killed five warriors and four women and two children before they were driven off," said Red Leggings.

"The horses are enclosed by a rope fence. And no one is watching them," said Buffalo Capture. "It is a good time to take the entire herd."

Red Leggings nodded and looked around the circle of faces huddled close, each man looking intently at him. With a calm voice, although his heartbeat was starting to quicken, he said, "Let us go without noise to the herd. When there, each take your rope and put it around the neck of your chosen horse, then loop it around his nose so he can be guided when ridden. Except Rides and Buffalo Capture, we will all remain on the south side of the enclosure with our captured horses in tow.

"Rides and Buffalo Capture will move to the north side, cut the rope fence, then give us the signal to move the herd out. Mount your horse and move the herd out slowly. We want to get as far from the camp as possible before they discover us. Let us pray that the Crows are heavy sleepers, and by the time they discover us, it will be too late, as they will have no horses left with which to chase us."

The moon was in the west, but gave enough light for their purposes. With braided rawhide ropes in hand, and their bows, arrows, and shields strung over their shoulders, Rides and Buffalo Capture moved cautiously around to the north side of the herd. Rides With Broken Leg clutched his medicine bag and silently prayed to Sound Of Wings.

Except for occasional shuffling of a horse, there was complete silence around the corral. The air had cooled enough that even the crickets were quiet.

"Did you hear that noise?" asked Buffalo Capture, his voice barely audible in a breathless whisper.

"What noise?"

"It sounded as if someone dropped something."

Rides whispered, "It was probably a horse moving."

When Rides and Buffalo Capture reached the north side of the herd, they slipped into the rope enclosure and moved stealthily toward the horses. They did not see the two ghostly figures on the opposite side of the herd. A few of the horses moved away, but most remained. Each man selected a horse and calmly whispered to the animal as he put a rope around its neck. Rides patted the neck and stroked the ears of his chosen mount, and it nickered.

They began to lead the two horses slowly and had nearly reached the fence when they both abruptly stopped. Rides whispered, "I heard someone running."

"So did I," agreed Buffalo Capture. "Listen."

With hearts pounding and ears straining, the two listened. No sound could be heard except their own breathing and the occasional sound of a horse. They quickly moved the next few steps to the fence. Knife in hand, Rides quietly cut the two strands of the rawhide rope fence. Buffalo Capture had mounted his horse.

Rides led his mount through the opening. He took its mane in his left hand and was ready to swing up, when he sensed rather than saw the figure coming at him. He swung around to the left with his arm still high. His buffalo-hide shield deflected the lance thrust at him and knocked it from the hand of his attacker. Rides' horse lunged and jerked the braided rope from his hand. As Rides pulled his knife from its sheath, he felt blood trickling down the exposed skin of his left shoulder. His assailant screamed and leapt at him. Rides' blood turned cold. It was "Half Ear."

Buffalo Capture was chasing a second Crow warrior. The Crow fell in his attempt to escape and was trampled by the horse of Buffalo Capture. In a flash, Buffalo Capture leapt from his mount and slashed the throat of his enemy. With the sharp point of his knife he cut a circle around the top of man's head, grabbed the slain enemy's hair with the other hand, put his foot against the man's neck and jerked the scalp loose as the man convulsed in death. Buffalo Capture pried the Crow knife out of the dying man's hand and thrust it in his own belt. With a fierce yell of victory, he remounted his horse, scalp in hand.

The scar on the neck of Half Ear seemed to bulge out in the moonlight, and the yellow glint of his eyes showed only hatred. The moonlight flashed off his knife as he lunged at Rides, who deftly sidestepped and let him pass. Half Ear crouched as he turned. He screamed something in Crow and charged. Rides ran backward a few paces, stepped to the side, and with his right foot tripped the man who fell face first.

Rides leapt at Half Ear and kicked at his face as he rolled over in the dirt. The kick caught the man's shoulder, but did not prevent him from cutting deeply into Rides' left shin. The Crow rolled over twice, trying to escape another kick, then rose and was nearly upright when Rides grabbed the man's knife hand and wrenched it behind his back. At the same instant, Rides cut deep into the man's throat. Blood spurted over the scar on Half Ear's neck as he gurgled and fell dying.

The herd began charging through the opening in the rope

fence, driven from behind by yells of the rest of the raiding party. The entire Crow village began to come alive. Shouts of confusion could be heard, then men began running toward the now nearly empty corral.

Rides quickly scalped Half Ear, cut off the remaining half of his left ear, and took the man's knife and belt. These he stuffed into his pouch as he ran looking for a path of escape. He felt pain in his left leg, but did not know the source. He yelled at a passing rider who seemed not to see him. Another rider came up beside him and yelled, "Grab my arm." He did, and Red Leggings pulled him up on his mount. They galloped away following the herd.

The horses were driven hard down the Yellowstone valley. As the sun was just beginning to brighten the eastern sky, the riders turned the herd north and were shortly out of the valley and among the rolling hills.

Red Leggings gave a command, and the riders brought the horses to a slow trot. He said to Rides, "It will be quite some time before the Crows can follow us. We did not steal all their horses, but it will take them some time to catch the ones remaining since they are scattered." He continued, "When the sun is fully in the sky, we will stop and rest for a short time. There we will catch a horse for you to ride."

The sun was above the horizon when Red Leggings gave the signal to halt in a small valley with a nearly dry stream. The mounts and the rest of the herd drank thirstily.

Rides dropped from the horse of Red Leggings – and nearly fell as pain seared his left leg as it touched the hard ground.

"What is wrong?" cried Red Leggings. "You have been wounded! Look at the blood on your leg! You also have blood on your arm and shoulder. How did it happen? Sit here by the stream and I will tend to your wounds." After he cleansed the injuries, Red Leggings took from his supply bag some powdered inner bark of the cottonwood tree. This was applied to the wounds to prevent further bleeding. He then bandaged the tender areas with white buckskin.

Rides told him of the fight with Half Ear and how he had come to be wounded. Then he opened the pouch for Red Leggings to see his trophies.

With Rides' wounds dressed and the herd watered, Red Leggings said, "We must move again," and motioned to Iron Man to bring a horse for Rides. Red Leggings boosted Rides onto the back of the new mount and remounted his own horse, as the herd began to move north.

They continued north at a trot all day, except to stop to allow the horses to drink and rest a short time when the sun reached its zenith. When they came over the hills which marked the southern boundary of the Musselshell River valley, the sun was low in the sky. The herd eagerly moved down the slope to the river.

"We will stop here and allow the horses to rest. Not long after sundown we will begin moving north again. The twilight should provide enough light until the moon rises. The going will be easy since we will be traveling down the valley," said Red Leggings.

After drinking, the herd began grazing the lush grasses along the stream. They would not need guarding or a rider to keep them from straying for some time. The men picketed their mounts to allow them to graze.

The flow of blood from Rides' wounds had stopped, but

they were now more painful. He walked with a half hop, and it was difficult for him to raise his left arm. All the warriors sat near the water's edge, drank the clear cold water, ate pemmican from their supplies, and talked excitedly of the raid, the number of horses stolen, and the fact that they had gotten away without anyone of their group being killed. "I counted them. We came away with forty-seven horses, including the ones we are riding," said Red Leggings.

At least three of the enemy were left dead. Besides the two killed by Buffalo Capture and Rides, Red Leggings had shot a Crow through the stomach with an arrow as the man ran toward the raiding party. Iron Man and Red Mane, bringing up the rear, had shot arrows at several pursuers but could not be sure if the arrows had hit their mark. Rides had been the only one wounded.

Rides lay down on the bank of the stream, hoping that in this position his leg would stop throbbing. It seemed to help, and he was dozing when Red Leggings gently shook him and said, "It is time to go. We will be safe when we have crossed the Missouri River." He helped Rides to his feet. Buffalo Capture held Rides' mount as he was boosted on its back by Red Leggings. "I know it is painful, my friend, but tomorrow night you can sleep in the lodge of your parents."

The victorious group moved the herd at an easy trot down the Musselshell valley. The next day, by the time the sun climbed to its high point, they had reached the confluence of the Missouri River. The horses were driven into the swift-moving water and swam across. As each rider urged his mount into the deep water, he slipped over its rump and grabbed the horse's tail, allowing himself to be pulled across the river by the swimming horse. Rides could hold the tail with his right hand only, but made the crossing safely.

The herd, pushed from behind by the men, wearily climbed the steep breaks of the northern valley wall. As his mount topped the valley, Rides With Broken Leg could see the Little Rocky Mountains only a half-day's ride to the north, and he felt at home. He put his hand on his medicine bag and thanked his guardian spirit.

The entire party stopped, turned their mounts to the south from whence they had come, and saw nothing moving except a few buffalo in the far distance. They were safe, well out of Crow territory. By the time the sun set, each would be in his own lodge.

A short distance from their village, Red Leggings called a halt. When everyone had dismounted, he said, "Here is some charcoal and a small amount of grease for each of you. Mix them together and paint each other's faces. When everyone from our village sees our black faces, they will know that our party was successful and had no losses."

Just before sunset they came in sight of their village. The village soldiers spotted them and alerted the entire village, which met and escorted them the remainder of the way. After much talking and laughing, the eight men were left to go to their lodges to eat and rest.

"My son, you are limping. Is it a bad wound?" asked Stands Alone.

"It is swollen, but does not seem to be too bad. It hurts to walk though. Red Leggings dressed it for me."

"Come to our lodge and we will call the herb doctor," said Wind Walker.

Old Fire and Blue Knife Woman both spoke at the same time, "We will go and get her."

Rides and his parents had hardly reached their lodge when the two adopted grandmothers arrived with the herb doctor.

"Look at his left arm, it is wounded also," said Old Fire. "Oh, my grandson, you have been badly hurt. Let me help you."

"I will take care of him now," interrupted the doctor. "I see, my grandson, that you have also been wounded in the leg. Do not worry, I will fix both your wounds." She took from her bag a sharp knife and cut off the bandages, inspecting the afflicted areas closely.

"There is some redness, but I have something to heal them." She produced the medicine. "I will apply this. It is made from the crushed root of the cattail and will reduce the redness around the wounds. First, let me wash them."

Afterwards, her job done, the doctor said, "Eat and sleep now, my grandson. Tomorrow you will feel much better."

The next day the chief of the soldiers announced that a Victory Dance would be held two days hence. The adopted grandmothers came to Wind Walker, and Old Fire said, "We will help prepare food for the dance for our grandson."

On the day of the celebration, Old Fire said, "I am so proud of him, and I am going to dance today in the Victory Dance."

"You are getting too old for that," replied Blue Knife Woman calmly as she continued to cut up the buffalo loin.

"I may be old, but not too old to dance for my grandson. He is so handsome and brave. He can also count many coups." She counted them off on her fingers, "The horses. The Crow's scalp, belt, and knife. As well as his half ear."

"I think we all should dance," said Wind Walker.

At mid-afternoon the dance began, led by the drumming and singing of three older men who had been great warriors.

The women formed a line on one side of the drummers, with the men on the other side. The drummers led the dance with songs of the deeds of the war party – how they managed to steal the horses from the Crow village. The women dancers carried the two scalps held high on long sticks.

Wind Walker carried the stick with the scalp of Half Ear and the knife her son had used to slay the man. The mother of Buffalo Capture carried the scalp of the Crow killed by her son. At the end of each song, they waved the scalps and held the weapons high for all to see. All the women carried and waved weapons of the type used in the raid.

"Wind Walker, I am so proud of my adopted grandson, would you let me carry the scalp and knife for one dance?" asked Old Fire.

"Please, take them."

The drummers began again. They sang of the killing of the Crow, Half Ear, by Rides With Broken Leg. Old Fire held the scalp high and shook it as she danced. Not a young woman anymore, she felt like she could dance forever as she thought about her adopted grandson's feats of bravery.

The dancing ended in late evening. All were invited to feasts given by the relatives of the warriors.

CHAPTER 10

"I do not believe he will ever come to our band to see you," said Blue Calf.

"Yes, he will. Rides With Broken Leg promised he would visit our band one day. I know he will be here soon," said Spotted Leg, though she was beginning to feel this was more a wish than reality.

"He could have found another girl and has forgotten you by now. It has been a long time since the Medicine Lodge Dance. Are you sure he really liked you?" asked her friend.

"I know he liked me. I could tell by the way he looked at me and how he talked. And it was *not* a long time ago. It has only been three moons since the dance," replied Spotted Leg.

"Even if he does come, what are you going to do about it? Your mother said your father has been approached by Black Cliff, who wants to marry you."

"I am not going to marry anyone now! I am not yet sixteen, and my father would not ask me to marry until I was at least that age. And if he said I should marry Black Cliff, I would refuse. I do not have to marry anyone I do not like. I might even run away to another band and take care of myself."

"But how would you live with no one to kill buffalo for you? You do not know how to shoot an arrow, let alone a gun.

And your father would come and find you."

"I could learn to hunt. And I would hide from my father," retorted Spotted Leg. She stopped cutting the buffalo meat which they were preparing for drying and held her knife high. Her large dark eyes flashed, and she looked directly at Blue Calf. "Rides With Broken Leg will come!"

"If he does come here to visit you, your father would not let you marry him anyway. He has nothing. No horses. No lodge. He hasn't been in any battles and cannot even count coups."

Holding back tears, Spotted Leg began, "I do not care what my father ..." when a commotion was heard nearby. They turned and saw several men looking to the north and talking excitedly. In the distance, three riders were moving slowly toward their village.

"It could be Rides With Broken Leg," said Blue Calf.

"Do not tease me. That is not funny."

"Oh, Spotted Leg, I really do hope it is he."

The two girls stopped cutting the meat, stood and watched. As the riders came nearer, Spotted Leg could not believe her eyes. Was it really the one she waited for?

She dropped the knife and grasped the hands of Blue Calf. "It is he! It is Rides With Broken Leg!" They started to jump up and down and dance in a circle.

"Stop! Stop! He will think we are children," said Spotted Leg suddenly. She resisted the urge to run as fast as her legs would carry her to meet the riders, to jump on the horse of Rides and hug him. That would not be dignified.

The girls left their work and moved behind the crowd that gathered. "Let us move up to the front so he can see you," whispered Blue Calf.

"I have blood and grease on my hands and clothes. We will stay in the back. I want to see him, but not for him to see me yet."

Someone in the crowd said, "I recognize two of them. One is Buffalo Capture, nephew of Wolf Hawk. And one is Rides With Broken Leg who danced in the Medicine Lodge Dance."

By the time the three reached the village, someone had summoned Wolf Hawk, who, as he came through the crowd, shouted, "Buffalo Capture! It is you! How happy I am to see you, my nephew. You look tired. Come, all of you. We will have food and drink while we talk." He led the three to his lodge.

"Rides With Broken Leg is so handsome," said Blue Calf.

"I know. I cannot wait to speak with him."

Wolf Hawk invited the three young men into his lodge. Before entering, they removed their weapons and medicine bags, placing them on a tripod near the lodge entrance.

As soon as the men had disappeared inside, Spotted Leg ran as fast as she could back to her lodge with Blue Calf on her heels.

Normally very polite, she shouted in her excitement, "Grandmother, grandmother, he is here! He is here! He and two others just rode into our village."

"Grandchild, what are you shouting about? Who is here?"

"Rides With Broken Leg. He is here! I must change my clothes. And clean the blood and grease from my hands and face. Help me, Grandmother."

"Grandchild, where is this boy and his friends now?"

"Wolf Hawk took them to his lodge. Buffalo Capture is Wolf Hawk's nephew."

"Then you have plenty of time to clean up and dress, for they will spend time eating and talking. I can also fix your hair. Now go and hang up the meat which you have cut for drying. Wrap the uncut part and hang it from one of the poles, out of reach of the dogs."

As Spotted Leg's grandmother predicted, the young warriors from the Little Rock Mountain Band spent time with Wolf Hawk and other guests, eating and exchanging news of their families. Buffalo Capture also told their hosts about the successful raid on the Crow village in which the three visitors had been involved. The three were then taken to the soldiers' lodge where they would remain as guests until the time of their departure.

"Does my hair look all right, grandmother?"

"Yes, my grandchild. It looks beautiful that way, pulled back and tied in the knot. Your dress also is very nice. And I have never seen that necklace before. Very pretty – a beaded piece of white buckskin tied tightly around your throat. It makes your face stand out. And brings out the sparkle in your eyes."

Spotted Leg was dressed in a soft white buckskin dress which came to just below her knees. The fringed elbow-length sleeves were decorated with dyed porcupine quills just above the fringes. Similar fringes and quills also graced the bottom of the dress. She wore white moccasins and fringed white leggings.

"Grandmother, do you think he will like me?"

"Spotted Leg, he will like you. Maybe too much."

"What does 'maybe too much' mean, grandmother?"

"It means that you are still very young. And your father may have plans for you other than this young boy."

"I am not very young. I am nearly sixteen. And father would

not make me marry anyone if I did not want the man."

"Grandchild, do not get too serious about this young man. Both of you could be very disappointed."

Blue Calf, nearly out of breath, ran into the lodge and blurted out, "Did you hear? I can hardly believe it. It is wonderful."

"What is it, my grandchild, what happened?"

"Rides With Broken Leg, he and ... oh, I can ... they ..."

"Slow down and catch your breath, child."

"My father told mother that Rides With Broken Leg and the others were on a raiding party against the Crow in the Yellowstone valley. They stole a large herd of horses. And Rides With Broken Leg killed a man who had half an ear. He also gained many coups."

"Blue Calf, who is this man with half an ear?" asked Spotted Leg.

"I am not sure, but they said something about a man who fought with the father of Rides With Broken Leg many years ago."

Rides With Broken Leg had tried to be patient during the feasting and storytelling. However, his purpose of coming to the Missouri River Dog Band village was not to eat, drink, and talk, but to see and speak with Spotted Leg. Just thinking about seeing her made his heart race.

"We have been sitting for a long time, Buffalo Capture. My left leg is getting stiff."

"Yes, we have been sitting long," responded Buffalo Capture, looking at their host, the chief of the village soldiers.

The chief said, "Please, you don't have to stay here for my

sake. Go for a walk about the camp. Food will be prepared for you again later."

The visitors left the soldiers' lodge. Rides With Broken Leg still limped slightly from the wound he had sustained. They walked in the direction of the late afternoon sun. The westerly breeze had subsided as the sun neared the horizon. Near the edge of the village, a lark celebrated the evening with its song. A dog barked, but Rides With Broken Leg saw or heard none of these things. They had not gone more than a few paces when the two girls stepped from behind a lodge a short distance ahead of the three.

They had not yet seen the young men. The setting sun was directly behind them, and they seemed to be looking at something near the horizon. One was pointing to the south. Her hair was tied in a knot. Her head was tilted back slightly. She was smiling. Seen in profile, the straight nose, full lips, slightly turned-up chin, and her slim, tall, gracefully proportioned body made Rides With Broken Leg feel as if he was dreaming. He would never forget that moment.

Looking into the sun, Rides could not see her face, but instinctively knew that it was Spotted Leg. He was reminded of the time he first had seen her. This afternoon, with the sunlight directly behind her, dressed all in white, she appeared again as a vision.

The vision slowly turned and looked directly at Rides who stood frozen.

"Greetings, Rides With Broken Leg. It is good to see you again. It is nice of you to visit our band."

Rides had visualized this moment and had many times practiced what he would say. He would greet and tell her how nice it was to see her again. Ask about her parents and their health. How was her grandmother? But all he could manage at that moment was, "Ah, well, ah ... hello." He did not see Blue Calf, and seemed oblivious to the other young men next to him, as he continued to stare at Spotted Leg.

"This is my friend, Blue Calf. What are the names of your friends, Rides With Broken Leg?"

"Oh, yes. This is Buffalo Capture. And Red Mane," Rides said, as his almost trance-like state broke. He continued, "Buffalo Capture came to your band to visit the family of his uncle, and asked me to join him."

"That was very nice of him to ask you to come along," said Spotted Leg. She was sure that Rides had given Buffalo Capture the idea of visiting her band.

"We have been sitting for quite some time and it is good to move about." Still looking directly at Spotted Leg, Rides asked, "Would you like to walk with us?"

"Thank you. That would be nice. You can tell me of your family and band." She knew that with the five people in their group, and with so many others about, the girls would not be required to have chaperones.

As they walked about the village, most of the discussion concerned things that had happened in the two bands since the time of the Medicine Lodge Dance.

"Rides With Broken Leg, you seem to be limping. Did you step on something or hurt your ankle?" asked Spotted Leg.

"No, I am fine. It is nothing," replied Rides as he tried to walk without the limp.

"Are you sure? It appears to be hurting you."

Buffalo Capture interrupted, "He is limping because of a

wound he got when fighting the Crow."

Rides began to protest, but at that moment a small child, who was playing tag with two other children, ran directly into Spotted Leg. She picked up the boy and handed him to Rides, who held him up and said, "Hello, young warrior. You look strong and well-fed."

Unsure what to do, the child stared at Rides, who patted his head and hugged him. The little boy smiled and began to giggle as he was put down. Rides laughed too. "Now go play, young warrior, but be careful." The boy ran off. "That one seems to have plenty of energy. What is his name?" asked Rides.

"His name is Spirit Water. You have seen him before – at the Medicine Lodge Dance. You may not remember, but he was the child that the woman brought to the medicine man when the dance was nearly finished," said Spotted Leg.

"Yes, I remember. The child appeared to be nearly dead."

"The water from the sacred center pole of the Medicine Lodge cured the boy. Because of that, he was given the name, Spirit Water."

The five young people walked around the entire village. Groups of women, working or visiting together, smiled and waved to them.

Blue Calf said, "Just look at their tongues wagging. We will not hear the end of this. Two girls of the Missouri River Dog Band walking with three boys of the Little Rock Mountain Band." Without thinking, she continued, "Spotted Leg, look! There is Black Cliff. He is staring at you with an evil look in his eye."

"He does not have an evil look. Anyway, what do I care about how he looks? It means nothing."

"Who is Black Cliff?" asked Rides.

"He is a man that likes Spotted Leg very much. I think –"

"He does not. Besides that, I do not like him. He seems unhappy and angry nearly all the time."

Rides looked at the man and could see the jealousy in his eyes. Black Cliff looked to be about twenty-five winters in age.

"But your father thinks –" Blue Calf began.

"Be quiet, Blue Calf. Leave my father out of this. I will do as I please."

"What about your father? Does he want you to marry this Black Cliff?" asked Rides.

"No, he does not. Blue Calf just thinks that. Besides, I do not want to talk about it anymore." Spotted Leg, looking at Rides, smiled and said, "Let us talk about more interesting things. Tell me what you have been doing since the Medicine Lodge Dance. Also I want to hear about the battle you were in with the Crows."

For Rides, the smile of Spotted Leg put Black Cliff out of his mind, but he somehow felt that it would not be for long.

The five walked around the camp until the sun began to set. The girls explained that they must go back to their lodges to help prepare the evening meal – and they could not be out with young men after sundown without a chaperone.

As they parted, Spotted Leg reached out and took the hand of Rides. "I have enjoyed walking with you. Maybe we can do this again before you leave."

The touch of her hand made a slight blush come over the face of Rides. "Thank you. Ah, yes ... I also hope that we can again walk together."

During the late afternoons of the next three days, the three young men and two girls strolled around the village, talking. Each day, Rides saw Black Cliff watching them.

Buffalo Capture also noticed Black Cliff, and said to Rides, "I do not like the look in his eye. Watch him closely."

As they walked on the last day before the three men were to depart, Rides and Spotted Leg moved a few paces ahead of the other three.

"I wish we could be alone for a short time. I have something I would like to tell you," said Rides.

"That can be arranged," said Spotted Leg. "Tonight after dark when everyone is in their lodges, give a signal, and I will come and meet you behind our lodge."

"But your parents will know."

"No, they will not, because I will tell them that the wind has changed and I must to go out and adjust the smoke flap or the lodge will be filled with smoke and no one will be able to sleep."

"What kind of signal should I give?"

"A whistle. Two short notes and one long note. No one will be suspicious. They will think it is children whose parents have not yet sent them to bed."

Later that evening, just as they had planned, Rides was waiting as Spotted Leg came out of the lodge. He took her hands, and they walked behind the lodge. In a whisper he said, "This is the first time we have been alone. You look beautiful."

"How can you tell? It is dark and you cannot see me."

"I can see you always in my mind and in my heart, and you are beautiful. I want to be your husband. I have loved you from the first time I saw you after the Medicine Lodge Dance."

"Yes, yes, I love you also and want to be your wife." She put her arms around his strong youthful frame.

Rides held her soft body tightly to his. "Next summer, when our bands come together for the Medicine Lodge Dance, I will speak with your father and present him with the appropriate gifts for you to become my wife."

In the darkness she looked at him. "I love you, Rides With Broken Leg. And I will be a good wife."

Their lips touched. "I must go before I am missed," she whispered, and was gone.

Rides was intoxicated with the magic of this night. He walked about the village, but never saw the millions of stars overhead, nor did he hear the owl calling in the distance. After a time, he found his way back to the soldiers' lodge where he slept fitfully.

Shortly after daybreak, Rides and his companions mounted their horses and bid farewell to Wolf Hawk and the others in the small group of well-wishers. As they were about to leave, Black Cliff came up to the edge of the group. He looked at Rides With Broken Leg and said, "Watch out for trouble."

He put his right forefinger to his throat and made a sign of cutting. Rides was the only person to see the sign since Black Cliff stood behind the others.

As they left the encampment of the Missouri River Dog Band, riding north toward their own village, Rides pondered the words of Black Cliff.

CHAPTER 11

Rides With Broken Leg could think of little else than Spotted Leg during the three-day journey back from the Missouri River Dog Band. On their return to the Little Rock Mountain Band, Rides and his companions were told that a Brave's Dance was to be held the next day. This dance was held at most two or three times a year and gave each warrior an opportunity to count his coups in the presence of the entire band.

Counting coups was the reenactment of deeds of valor. These included being one of the first four warriors to strike or touch a downed enemy, taking a possession of an enemy, taking a scalp, stealing horses, being wounded by an enemy, firing a gun more than ten times during a battle, striking a lodge in the enemy camp with anything held in the hand, and killing a grizzly bear alone and on foot.

Killing an enemy from a distance did not count since it did not take bravery. However, to touch an enemy or take one of his possessions was especially dangerous since he might be pretending to be dead and could retaliate. The first to touch the enemy counted two coups. The next three to touch the man could count one coup each. Likewise, the other feats of bravery counted one coup for each act.

During the dance, the warrior carried the actual weapons

or an item to represent the implements used in the deeds being depicted.

Old Fire, adopted grandmother of Rides With Broken Leg, was among the first to see the young man ride back into the village. "My grandson, I am so happy that you have returned. You must prepare yourself for the dance tomorrow. After the dance, we will make a great feast for you. We will have all of your favorite foods."

"Grandmother, I am not sure that I should participate in the dance. My leg is still not very strong." His mind was far from dancing. If only Spotted Leg were here, he could dance the night through and all the next day. Why had he not eloped with her that night when they met behind her lodge? They could have been gone before anyone would have noticed.

"Grandson, you must participate. Your father will dance. You must dance with him. You have seen him count coups before. He will be proud to have you with him the first time you count coups."

When he reached the lodge of his parents, he found that Wind Walker had made a new pair of moccasins for him. The coyote tails sewn to the heels showed that he had stolen horses. An eagle feather lay across the moccasins. This would be worn in his hair, a sign that he had killed an enemy. Alongside were his father's moccasins, which were similar except that several eagle feathers lay on them. And in spite of his worries about his injured leg, Rides was proud to join in his first Brave's Dance.

The dance began shortly before noon. The singers with drums were four older men. Eight women, including Old Fire and Blue Knife Woman, stood behind the men and sang along with them. Only men participated in the dancing. They wore nothing but moccasins and a breech-clout, and they danced in a circle. After each round was completed, another warrior moved into the center of the group and reenacted his courageous deeds during battle.

Rides' father, Stands Alone, counted his many coups, including his earlier fight with the Crow known as Half Ear. When he was finished, another round was danced. The music stopped, and then Rides With Broken Leg moved into the center of the circle.

Rides held out his arms and said, "Four moons ago, in the company of seven others, many Crow horses were stolen." In response, the drummers tapped once in unison.

Rides continued. "I fought with the Crow, Half Ear, and was first to touch him." The drum sounded twice. Rides took out his knife and reenacted the entire battle, demonstrating how he had cut the man's throat. The drummers tapped in reply.

"Before the enemy was dead, I took his scalp." The drummers tapped. "I then took his knife ..." the drummers tapped again, "as well as his belt." Yet another beat was struck.

Rides pointed to the scar on his shoulder. While walking completely around the inside of the circle, he said, "In this fight, I was wounded in the shoulder by the enemy lance." The drumbeat rang out. Then he pointed to his shin, "Also, the enemy knife cut me in this spot." Again the drum sounded.

Rides looked at his father and saw the pride in his eyes. Rides continued, "To show that he was the man with whom my father fought, I cut off his half ear." The drummers gave one last beat.

Rides had completed his coup count, and another round was danced. Then the next warrior entered the circle. By the time each warrior had counted his coups, the sun was low in the west. After the dance ended, the relatives of the men who had participated were ready to host a feast in celebration.

"Grandson, you were so handsome as you counted coups. I am so proud of you. Let us eat," said Old Fire.

CHAPTER 12

It was in the evening during the last days of *Tabehatawe*, Frog's Moon (April), that Old Fire, his adopted grandmother, spoke to him. "Grandson, do you remember the feast we gave for you after the last Medicine Lodge Dance? Afterwards, a girl – who I think you liked very much – came to see you. Spotted Knee, I believe, was her name."

"Spotted Leg, grandmother," corrected Rides With Broken Leg.

"Yes, yes, Spotted Leg. Oh, I remember we had such a good time – and the food! How I remember the food."

"Yes, grandmother the food was very good, but you were going to tell me something about Spotted Leg."

"My cousin and her family from the Missouri River Dog Band have been here visiting. She is a friend of the mother of Spotted Leg. She said that the girl may be married soon. Her father has been approached by a man in that band. I cannot remember his name. It something like Dark Rock. Black Rock, or something like that."

Rides felt panic in his stomach. He thought he would be sick. He swallowed hard and lied, "If she wants to marry him, I hope that they will have many children and be happy."

"My cousin said that the girl has not yet agreed to marry

this Black Cliff – yes, that is his name. He owns many horses and guns, and the gifts he gives to the father of Spotted Leg will be many. Of course the father cannot force her to marry anyone. However, he is said to be very persuasive, and the girl will probably consent to the marriage."

Rides thoughts tumbled over each other. He knew that Spotted Leg loved *him*, not Black Cliff. She had promised to marry him! He must do something. He had to speak with her.

No! He would speak with her father. But her father would refuse any proposal that Rides put forth. Rides With Broken Leg was not wealthy, like Black Cliff.

He could kill Black Cliff. No, that would not work either. Rides would probably be killed in retaliation by his rival's family. Suddenly, he knew what he had to do.

When his adopted grandmother left, Rides went immediately to the lodge of the soldiers. He inquired of the location of the Missouri River Dog Band. He was told that at last contact, the band was east of the Larb Hills. By now they might be moving toward the Three Buttes, near where the Medicine Lodge Dance was to be held this year. By the time he left the lodge, a plan had formulated in his mind.

Rides With Broken Leg found Buffalo Capture and told him about his plan to steal away Spotted Leg. Buffalo Capture tried to talk him out of it, saying that it could not be done. He pointed out that there was not any way that Rides could enter her village without being known to nearly everyone, especially Black Cliff.

"Then I must kill Black Cliff."

"You may kill him, but you would still not get the girl. And her relatives and the relatives of Black Cliff would see to it that you were soon dead as well."

"Spotted Leg promised to marry me. I know that she does not love Black Cliff. You saw how she acted when he stared at her. I must stop this marriage!" Desperation shone in his eyes.

"Maybe I can help you," said Buffalo Capture. "I have an idea which I believe will work."

"No! I cannot let you get involved. If there is a chance I may be killed, it could happen to you also if you help me."

"No one will be killed. Before you make a decision, let me explain my plan."

The two young men informed their parents that they were going to visit the uncle of Buffalo Capture, and before dawn the next morning, they were riding toward the rising sun. When the sun had reached its high point in the sky, they stopped by one of the few streams they had seen that morning. The horses were watered and put on pickets to graze. The men drank and washed in the cool water. After eating some of the dried buffalo meat which each carried, they filled their water bags made from buffalo stomachs, then remounted and continued in an easterly direction at a full trot.

Late in the afternoon of the second day, they spotted smoke in the distance. This could only be from cooking fires of the Missouri River Dog Band. The two turned south and rode a short distance to a small pine-covered ridge. From this vantage point, the village could be observed without the two being seen. They dismounted and ate from their provisions while discussing the plan to steal away Spotted Leg.

"I will try to be back shortly before sundown," said Buffalo

Capture as he remounted and rode off toward the village. Rides nodded and with a quick wave of his hand, settled down to wait.

After exchanging greetings with several of the elders and soldiers, Buffalo Capture was directed to the lodge of his uncle. They ate, smoked, and visited. After a while, Buffalo Capture casually asked about the health of Blue Calf and Spotted Leg, the two young women with whom he and the other young men had visited the previous year.

His uncle hesitated and looked at his wife for help. She said that the health of the two was fine. However, Spotted Leg was to be married.

According to the girl's grandmother, who lived with Spotted Leg and her parents, the marriage would take place shortly after sundown that very evening.

The Nakota had no fixed ceremony of marriage. It was considered a civil rather than a religious matter. A man wanting to marry sent an elder of the band as an emissary to the parents of the chosen girl, informing them of his desire. The parents could reject the offer and nothing further would be done. If they accepted, they must then get consent of the daughter.

If she did not consent, she was not forced to marry. However, if the suitor was prominent in the community and very well-to-do, the parents would try very hard to persuade the girl to change her mind. They knew that they would receive many presents, and have someone to hunt and provide meat for them in the future.

Once the girl gave her consent, the parents arranged a time for the marriage. When that time came, the bride cooked some meat. Accompanied by the elder who had arranged the marriage, she took the meat to the lodge of the bridegroom. As they approached, the elder announced in a loud voice, "I am coming home," indicating that the lodge was now the home of the girl. The elder entered, followed by the bride. The elder sat down on the right side of the groom, and the bride on the groom's left. Across from them sat the parents of the groom.

Four pieces of the meat cooked by the bride were placed in a single bowl and eaten by the couple. Once each had eaten two pieces, they drank from one bowl of water.

After this, the elder spoke to the groom. He was told to love his wife, provide plenty of good food, and protect her at all times from any danger. He was not to be jealous and should never strike his wife. Once finished with the lecture, the elder would say, "Grandson, this is now your wife. What is yours now belongs also to her. She will live in your lodge, and share your fire and food. Love her and share your life with her, and you will be blessed with healthy children and long life. Her parents are now your parents. Respect them, and treat them as your own."

To the bride, the elder would say, "Granddaughter, this is now your husband. What is yours is now your husband's, and what is his now also belongs to you. Keep your lodge clean, prepare his food on time. Love and respect his parents as your own, for they will be of great aid to you at all times."

The parents of the groom were entreated to love the bride as their own daughter and to give aid and support to the couple at all times.

The newlyweds would live with either his or her parents for the first year or so. If they lived with the bride's parents, the groom was expected to provide meat for her parents as well as to help out in other ways.

The sun was low in the west when Buffalo Capture returned to the pine ridge. Rides was pacing back and forth.

"I was beginning to believe you had forgotten I was still here," said Rides.

"I had not forgotten. However, it was difficult to explain to my uncle that I had to ride back out of camp when I had just arrived!"

Rides hardly heard what was said. "Did you see her? Is she married yet? Where is her lodge? Can I get to it without being seen?"

"You are talking too fast. Let me explain everything to you slowly."

Buffalo Capture explained that the marriage would take place that evening, shortly after sundown. Their plan must be executed right at sunset, when Spotted Leg would be in her lodge cooking the meat to be eaten at the ceremony. Buffalo Capture carefully described the layout of the village, the location of his uncle's lodge and its markings, and the location of the lodge of Spotted Leg. Rides remembered well the markings on her lodge from their last visit.

The two rode together at a relaxed pace into the village from the west. With the setting sun behind them, it would be difficult for any suspicious person to recognize Rides With Broken Leg. However, the two had little to worry about. Most of the men were visiting in small groups discussing a coming buffalo hunt. The women were at cooking fires, preparing the evening meal, and children seemed to be everywhere, playing games.

Entering the village, they stepped from their horses and led them. As they walked, Buffalo Capture said, "My friend, I wish you luck and pray that your guardian spirit will help you in this plan. Now I must leave you and return to the lodge of my uncle, or they will come searching for me. I will be waiting to hear that you have been successful in what you now are about to do."

He turned and in a moment was swallowed up by a throng of playing children that dashed in front of Rides' view.

Rides approached the lodge of Spotted Leg from the rear. When within about three paces he stopped and casually turned to look in the direction from which he had come. No one was following. He listened, but with the children playing in the background, no sound could be heard coming from the lodge.

As he began to move slowly past the lodge, he heard a muffled sob from within. A sympathetic voice said, "Please, granddaughter, do not cry. Your marriage is for the best. Black Cliff will make a good husband, and he will provide for your parents in their old age. You will see."

"But grandmother, I do not love him."

"I know! You love that boy from the other band. If I could give him to you as a present, I would do it now." The words had hardly escaped her mouth when Rides stepped through the entrance of the lodge.

Spotted Leg was kneeling in front of the small fire, cooking meat for the marriage ceremony. The grandmother stood behind the girl with a hand on her shoulder. The parents of Spotted Leg were nowhere to be seen.

The girl saw him and flew to her feet. With tears streaming down her face, she took two steps and fell into the arms of her love, nearly knocking him backwards. The grandmother stood frozen as the two embraced, then said, "What are you doing here? No one, especially a man, should be in this lodge except Spotted Leg and me. You must leave. She is preparing the meat for her marriage which is to take place very shortly."

Rides looked into the eyes of Spotted Leg. "I'm taking you away from this place now."

There was not time for a reply as Blue Calf, the best friend of Spotted Leg, stepped through the lodge entrance. "I heard a man's –" She stared at Rides in disbelief. Her face broke into a smile. "I had hoped you would come, but I never believed it would happen. The two of you must leave immediately. In a short time, the elder will come to escort Spotted Leg to the marriage ceremony."

"You cannot leave," said the grandmother. "You have been promised, and you have consented to marry Black Cliff."

Her eyes were filled with tears as Spotted Leg replied, "Please, grandmother, I could never be a good wife to that man."

"We do not have time to discuss this. Let us leave now," demanded Rides.

"But if you leave they will see you and bring you back. You could not get away," responded the grandmother.

Looking at the grandmother, Blue Calf broke in, "If we help, I know how they can escape without being seen. They will be far from the village before anyone knows that they are gone."

The sun had set. An old woman, with a long dark blanket pulled tightly about her head and face, walked toward the edge of the village. Hunched over and walking with a limp, she was assisted by her grandson who wore a black cloth tied about his head.

At the same moment, the elder stood outside the lodge of Spotted Leg and said, "Granddaughter, your future husband awaits. Let us go to the lodge of his parents for the marriage ceremony."

The bride stepped from the lodge. Her knee-length white buckskin dress stood out in the twilight. It was decorated with colored porcupine quills around the neckline, sleeves, and just above the bottom fringes. The sleeves were also adorned with small delicate fringes. White moccasins and white leggings completed the wedding attire. A white shawl covered her head, and she carried a wooden bowl of freshly cooked meat. She nodded to the elder, but kept her head bowed.

As they moved away, the girl's grandmother stepped from the lodge.

"Granddaughter, now remember – do not hurry. A bride should walk slowly. Take plenty of time. Let everyone in the village see your beautiful dress."

The three walked slowly in the direction of the lodge of the groom, the elder leading the way, the grandmother in the rear. They had passed several lodges when the bride turned to the right, away from the direction they had been heading. Surprised, the elder asked, "Where you going?" He received no reply, but could only turn and follow the bride. The three, with the bride leading, walked slowly about the nearly eighty lodges. This took a considerable time. People, especially women and children, came out from nearly every lodge to bid happiness to the bride. Many joined in and followed the procession.

Twilight was fading when they turned finally in the direction of the lodge of the groom. The openings at the tops of the many lodges along the way were illuminated from within with what seemed to be a romantic light.

When the lodge of the groom was reached, the procession stopped. The elder stepped in front of the bride, and in a loud voice said, "I am coming home." He hesitated, then stepped through the entrance to the lodge, followed by the bride. Those following the procession turned and went back to their lodges. The grandmother waited a moment, then moved around the outside of the lodge to the rear. The smile on her face was hidden by darkness.

Black Cliff sat with his head down as the two entered. His parents sat with their backs to the entrance. The elder moved around the parents and took his place on the right of Black Cliff. The bride moved to the left side of the groom, and knelt beside him. She removed her shawl. As it dropped behind her, Black Cliff, with his head still lowered, heard a gasp from his parents. He looked up, saw the surprise in their faces, and turned to look at the smiling Blue Calf.

Rage shone in his eyes and twisted his face as Black Cliff swung his left hand backward and slapped the face of the unsuspecting Blue Calf. The blow knocked her backward, but she remained upright. The smile never left her face as blood trickled from her nose and mouth.

Black Cliff leaped to his feet and demanded, "Where is she? Where is Spotted Leg?"

"My grandson, why ...?" said the elder. He was ignored.

"She has gone, and you will never find them." Blue Calf immediately regretted the words.

"What do you mean, never find *them*? She is with another man? I will not only find them, I will kill them. Who is the man? Is it Rides With Broken Leg?"

"I would never tell you!"

Black Cliff raised his hand ready to strike again. He stared into the eyes of Blue Calf. "I should kill you. Where have they gone?"

With blood dripping from her chin, she looked directly into his eyes and said nothing.

In the meantime, the "old woman" and her "grandson" who had left the camp just before the ceremony began had ridden due west until they were lost in the twilight. At that point, Spotted Leg, sitting behind Rides, cast off the blanket covering her head and hugged the man she loved.

"We are free!" she said. In her joy, she did not notice the scarlet ribbon that fell from her hair to the ground when the blanket was removed.

Rides With Broken Leg, with the arms of Spotted Leg tightly entwined about him, turned the horse and galloped in a south-easterly direction toward the Missouri River.

CHAPTER 13

Dawn was breaking as Black Cliff left the village of the Missouri River Dog Band. Riding one horse and leading another, he galloped west. He believed that Rides With Broken Leg, with Spotted Leg, would be returning to the safety of his own band. If he were to catch them before they reached the Little Rock Mountain Band, he must ride very fast. This was the reason for two horses. When the horse being ridden began to tire, he would ride the other and lead the first.

He would have asked one or more friends to accompany him, except for his humiliation and anger. His eyes became slits at the thought of the pleasure he would have in killing Rides With Broken Leg, who had been a thorn in his side since Black Cliff first saw that young man walking with Spotted Leg. As for Spotted Leg – Black Cliff still wanted her, but knew that he must kill her too, or he would be the laughing stock of the band.

Had he left earlier, before dawn, he would have missed the only clue to the direction taken by his prey. He would have missed it anyway, had not the scarlet ribbon been in such sharp contrast with new green grass which had sprouted in the past few days.

He stopped his horse and stepped down. Picking up the

ribbon, he examined the ground closely. He saw that a horse had turned sharply and headed toward the southeast. After walking a few paces, the man remounted and rode at a gallop in the direction the tracks led.

In the safety of their hiding place, Spotted Leg opened her eyes and smiled when Rides touched her hand. But he put his forefinger to his lips, a sign for silence. "Someone is coming," he whispered.

"My father could not have found us this soon," she whispered, searching his eyes. "Maybe it is Black Cliff."

They were near the north side of the Missouri River, in a small grassy area surrounded by willows which concealed them from view. Picketed nearby, their horse looked up at them, then continued to graze. It was now early afternoon. This spot had been their refuge since shortly after sunrise. The morning had been chilly, but the lovers never noticed the cold as they lay together, rolled in the old woman's blanket.

"I heard the sound of trotting horses coming this way. I think that there are two. Wait here." Rides moved quickly to the edge of the clearing and peered through the willows. He returned to Spotted Leg, a sober look on his face. "It is Black Cliff. He is very near and moving this way. I think he has seen our tracks. Come and hide in the willows," he whispered.

They moved to a point where they could observe their enemy, but could not be seen by him. Black Cliff came on steadily, but had slowed his horse to a walk and was carefully surveying the tracks which were leading him directly toward the willow grove.

Rides motioned Spotted Leg to remain hidden. He moved into position behind a large cottonwood tree for a surprise attack on their pursuer. The back of his left hand was pressed against the tree to steady his aim as he waited for Black Cliff to come into view. Rides' bow string was pulled to its limit when the enemy appeared.

At that instant a gun shot rang out, followed by shouting. Startled, Rides instinctively released the arrow, but his aim had been thrown off. The arrow hit the left shoulder of the trailing horse being led by Black Cliff. The animal snorted and reared in pain. The unsuspecting rider was jerked from his mount by the long braided rawhide rope used to lead the extra horse.

The coiled rope, which had been thrown over Black Cliff's shoulder to allow freedom of his hands, became entangled in his feet as he fell. The wounded horse began running, with Black Cliff being dragged behind, directly at the tree behind which Rides was stationed. As the panicked animal approached, Rides stepped from behind the tree. The horse veered to the side, but the force generated by the turn slammed Black Cliff into the tree with a sickening thud. The man was dead on impact. The body was dragged for another hundred paces before the rope broke.

Rides ran to where Black Cliff lay, with another arrow notched and ready to fire. But one quick look assured him that the man who lay crumpled on the ground would never again be a problem to anyone.

Once released from the burden of dragging the man, the horse came to a stop, turning his head and licking the wound from which the arrow still protruded. Rides, speaking softly, approached the animal. He took hold of the remaining part of the rope and held the horse firm. He did not want their position given away to whomever had fired the gun shot that had startled the beast. He patted the neck of the animal and examined the feathered projectile in its shoulder. The soft speech and patting calmed the horse. Rides rubbed the shoulder and slowly moved his hand to the arrow. He grasped the shaft and jerked it out of the flesh of the animal. The beast snorted and shied away, but the man held fast to the rope.

In the meantime, Spotted Leg had led Black Cliff's other horse into their sanctuary. She motioned to Rides to keep silent. He quickly led the wounded animal into the sheltered area as well.

Together, they crept to a point where they could observe the nearby Missouri River through the willows without being seen. Two boats were moving slowly upriver, while a third vessel slid to shore on the opposite bank to claim the large whitetailed deer which had been killed by the gun shot.

"Look," whispered Spotted Leg, "most have hair on their faces. They must be white men. I have never seen white men before, but I have heard that they have hair on their faces. There are at least forty, maybe more. But the woman in front of the largest canoe – she is not one of them. She is pointing the way. Look, she has a baby. And see the man standing behind her? He does not have hair on his face."

"The woman is not a Nakota," said Rides. "Nor is she from any other nation near here. If she were, I would recognize the way she is dressed. She may be from the Big Mountains, far to the west. Look at the size of the largest canoe. It must be fifteen or twenty paces in length! I wish Buffalo Capture were here to see this."

The deer was loaded into the small vessel pulled up onto the far shore, which then rejoined the other two craft moving up the river. The couple watched fascinated as the boats moved laboriously against the current. Who were these white men? Where were they going? Why so many?*

For the moment, the dead man lying nearby had been forgotten.

Once the boats were out of sight, reality returned. Spotted Leg asked, "What are we going to do with Black Cliff?"

"We will bury him here. He does not deserve being put in the tree tops."

Rides went to the wounded horse and examined the spot from which the arrow had been removed. He cleansed the wound with water from the river. The horse was in some pain, but the wound would heal quickly.

Rides found a curved tree branch and scraped a shallow pit in the soft earth of the river bottom. There they dragged the body of Black Cliff and rolled it into the pit to be covered with soil, on top of which branches were placed.

"Let us leave this place of death," said Rides as he moved toward the horses.

The lovers followed the river downstream. Spotted Leg rode their horse, while Rides With Broken Leg rode Black Cliff's

. . . .

* The Lewis and Clark Expedition reached the mouth of the Musselshell River on May 2, 1805, and reported seeing abandoned Assiniboine camps and other signs of native people having been in the area. Guided by the woman Sacajawea, of the Shoshone people – a tribe which lived west of the Rocky Mountains – the exploring party passed by without stopping on their long journey to discover a route to the Pacific Ocean.

horse and led the wounded animal.

They crossed the Milk River near its confluence with the Missouri, then headed north. On the third day, near Woody Mountain (present-day Wood Mountain in Canada, just north of the U.S. border), the two lovers reached their goal: the village of the Paddlers of the Prairie Band.

CHAPTER 14

When Rides With Broken Leg and Spotted Leg arrived at the band of the Paddlers of the Prairie, they were met by two soldiers at the edge of the village. Rides made the sign of recognition. He imitated paddling a canoe, first on one side, then on the other.* The soldiers returned the sign and welcomed the young couple into the village. They were taken to the guest lodge and given food.

The two lovers explained to the soldiers that they had eloped and needed to stay with this band for several months before they could return to the band of Rides' parents. The soldiers understood their situation and invited the young couple to a feast that evening to celebrate an upcoming buffalo hunt.

At the feast, the soldiers introduced Rides to many of the men. A young women, carrying a baby, introduced herself to Spotted Leg. Her name was Glittering Spring. Mutual admiration was immediate between the two women. Spotted Leg's beauty and happy, outgoing manner were nearly matched by

---

* The Paddlers of the Prairie Band were also known as the Prairie Assiniboine. The "sign of recognition," imitating the paddling of a canoe, may have been a carryover from the days when the tribe inhabited the lakes region of Minnesota, more than two hundred years earlier.

that of Glittering Spring. Before the feasting and celebrating was over that night, the two were fast friends.

The first buffalo hunt of the season, involving the entire band, would take place in three days. The medicine man had called the hunt shortly after scouts had reported spotting a herd of about one thousand buffalo moving in the direction of the village – the first great herd of the spring.

Each year in the late fall and winter, the buffalo separated into small groups and moved south and southeast for better forage. Each spring, when the new grass began to flourish, the animals reassembled in great masses, and moved north and northwest for the summer. Each Nakota band, typically eighty to one hundred lodges, also separated into small groups during the winter. It was much easier for a small group of only eight to fifteen lodges to find enough game to sustain themselves through the long cold prairie winter.

For the next two days, as the large herd approached the village, the scouts had kept track of its location. In the meantime, the soldiers who kept order in the village organized the hunt, assembling a group of seventy-two hunters. About half were on horses and the rest on foot. Just after sunrise on the morning of the hunt, the entire village, except for the elderly and infants, were led out of the village by the scouts and soldiers. They moved toward the southeast.

The men of the village went first. The women followed, some riding horses pulling a travois, others walking, followed by dogs also pulling travois. These sled-like carriers, with long poles hitched to the animals, would be used to carry meat and hides back to the village.

Spotted Leg, riding one horse and leading a second, said,

"Look at my husband, Rides With Broken Leg, on his buffalo horse. He is so handsome. I hope he will kill many animals today, because we need the hides so I can make a lodge for us for the winter. I will be glad to move out of the guest lodge into our own place."

Glittering Spring, riding beside Spotted Leg, replied, "Yes, he is handsome. If he does not kill enough buffalo to make a lodge, we will give some hides to you. And I will help you make your lodge."

The sun had hardly moved above the horizon when they spotted the lead animals of the herd.

A breeze had not yet risen, and the buffalo had no clue that humans were anywhere in the vicinity. The scouts gave a signal, and the soldiers motioned the entire group to move back to a small dry stream valley which they had just crossed. Here they would wait, concealed, until the herd was very near.

With the group concealed, the scouts again signaled the soldiers, who motioned to the hunters to follow them. The scouts led the way, racing toward the herd, with the soldiers and other mounted hunters following. The riders quickly encircled about five hundred animals. The remainder of the herd was allowed to go free.

This was known as the surround method of killing buffalo. The surround was a very efficient way of slaughtering many animals in a short time by mounted hunters as well as men on foot. And since all of the animals would be felled in a very small area, this method made for very efficient butchering.

The herd stampeded, but the riders moved in immediately and turned them to run in a circle, driving them always to run in a direction so that it was easiest for a right-handed man, chasing the galloping animals, to hold his bow and shoot to his left from his horse, without having to twist in his saddle.

Chasing buffalo in the surround was dangerous, and a hunter's buffalo horse had to be a very well-trained animal. The horse had to move in close to the running animals, guided only by the man's knees, since the man needed both hands free to shoot. The horse had to be alert and not trip over any fallen animals. A fall could be fatal for horse and rider. Because of the training required, some horses were used exclusively for buffalo hunting by their owners.

Once the animals were running in a circle, the mounted men, each carrying only a bow and arrows, began shooting the buffalo from short range, perhaps only three to five paces away. Their goal was to sink one arrow into the beast just behind the shoulder. They would then move to another animal and repeat the process. Each animal into which an arrow had been driven might not die immediately, but would surely succumb by the time the hunt was over.

When the men on the ground reached the herd, the buffalo had made one complete circle. Each of these men carried one or more guns. When they were about fifty paces from the stampede, they knelt down and began shooting.

The mounted men did not use guns, because after firing a shot, it was difficult and time-consuming to reload while seated on a running horse. However, the men on the ground could easily aim, fire, and take the time to reload.

Rides With Broken Leg had notched an arrow on his bow-string just before the riders moved out of the valley. He and Gray Horn, husband of Glittering Spring, were near the end of the group of mounted hunters as they moved toward the herd.

The first buffalo near enough for him to shoot was a calf. He rode past this animal and sunk an arrow instead into a young bull. Right after the arrow penetrated, the bull snorted and blood blew from his nose. He took a few more steps and turned over. Several beasts running behind the bull could not veer away soon enough and fell over the young bull. One broke its leg, and another broke its neck. Rides' buffalo horse had to leap over two other animals on the ground to avoid falling and being trampled by the herd, and Rides was nearly thrown.

Once he and his horse recovered, Rides shot an old bull, but the arrow hit the shoulder blade and did little damage. By the time he notched another arrow, a young cow was not more than four paces in front and to his left. Her skin would make a very good robe for the coming winter. He let the arrow fly. It penetrated the heart and the animal immediately fell dead.

The herd had not completed more than ten circles when a halt was called to the hunt. The mounted men had used most of their arrows, and more than two hundred animals lay dead or dying. The remainder of the buffalo in the surround were let go to join the main herd which had stampeded away to the north.

The medicine man and the chief of the soldiers moved to the center of the circle. All around lay the slaughtered buffalo. The medicine man, followed by the soldiers' chief, moved to each of the animals. The medicine man touched each buffalo with a wand of braided sweetgrass and thanked the spirit of each for giving up its life. Then he thanked Wahkonda for providing the buffalo for the Nakota. When he had finished, he signaled to the waiting families, and the butchering began.

In the Nakota society, there was a very sharp division of

labor between men and women. However, butchering buffalo after a kill was shared equally by all, including children. It could generally be determined by the arrow in an animal to which hunter the animal belonged. Each hunter had personal markings on his arrows. If there was a dispute, it was settled immediately by the soldiers. Generally, there were more than enough animals to go around, and everyone had plenty of meat and skins.

If it were to be used for a robe, the skin of the animal was removed in two pieces. The buffalo was slit down the stomach and also down the backbone. If it was to be used for making a lodge, the animal was slit down the stomach and the skin was removed in one large piece. The meat was cut from the bones and temporarily stored on the hide.

The tongue, brains, heart, liver, stomachs, and most of the intestines were also carefully removed from the animal and placed on the hide.

The tongues, considered a delicacy, were saved for the soldiers, who had the first choice of various parts of the animal. The brains were eaten or used in tanning hides. Stomachs were dried and used for water bags, or boiled and eaten. It was said by the hunters that to eat some of the liver raw would ensure good luck in the next hunt. By the time the sun had reached its zenith, nearly half of the buffalo had been butchered.

Rides With Broken Leg had killed eight buffalo, not including the one that broke its neck in the fall. After the medicine man had finished his prayers, Spotted Leg joined Rides. The two worked together to butcher their animals.

"My love, you were so handsome and brave as you raced around the herd. I was so proud to call you my husband."

"My wife, all the animals I killed were for you. I hope that the skins will be enough to make our own lodge. I want to live with you in our own place, and not be dependent on the band for our lodging."

By the time the sun was low in the west, and purple and red rays filled the sky, the butchering was completed. The meat and skins of the animals killed by Rides were loaded onto the travois of the two horses brought by Spotted Leg for the slow return trip to the village.

The medicine man left a scarlet cloth on a staff near the center of the surround as a tribute to the spirit of the buffalo. The entire group returned to the village where feasting and dancing continued throughout the night. No one, except Glittering Spring and Gray Horn, seemed to notice the new young couple slip off to the guest lodge before midnight.

CHAPTER 15

Three days after the hunt, the women and girls prepared the buffalo hides for tanning. Any meat and fat remaining on the hide was scraped off with a hoe-shaped tool made from the horn of an elk. The hides were then stretched out to dry. Small holes were cut in the edges, and pegs were put through the holes and driven into the ground to keep the hides taut. The hides would be dry in several days. In the winter, because of snow or frozen ground, the hides were stretched on racks especially made for this purpose.

The women began the process of cutting the meat for drying. This was a good time for the women to catch up on all the latest news and gossip of the village.

Though only sixteen, Spotted Leg had been trained in the skills needed for a wife. She had never constructed a lodge by herself, but Glittering Spring and many other women of the Paddlers of the Prairie Band volunteered to assist her. The women all wanted to hear the story of her elopement, and Spotted Leg told of their harrowing flight from the village of the Missouri River Dog Band on the eve of her planned marriage to Black Cliff.

She also told them of the mystery of the party of white men, guided by an Indian woman with a baby, moving up the

Missouri River in three very large canoes. This would be the talk of the village in the coming days.

"I miss my grandmother, and my mother," Spotted Leg confided to Glittering Spring. "Grandmother is getting old and may not live much longer, but I am afraid to go back to my band. My father would be very angry and may want to kill my husband." Tears filled her eyes.

"He will get over his anger in time. Besides, you cannot marry Black Cliff anyway now that he is dead."

The women cut the meat into long thin strips and hung it on ropes or poles to dry. In this very dry climate, the meat would be ready to be put away in a few days, packed in buckskin bags for future use. The dried meat could later be boiled or roasted. Sometimes, it was pounded directly into a powder, mixed with rendered tallow, and made into cakes which were eaten raw. However, it was generally made into pemmican, for which the Nakota were well-known throughout the region. To make pemmican, the women first roasted and then pounded the meat, then mixed it with pounded juneberries or cherries and a small amount of rendered tallow. This mixture was then formed into a patty. It made a tasty, nutritious snack or meal all in itself, and was easily stored and carried.

By the time all the meat was cut and put out to dry, the hides would be dry and ready for tanning.

Spotted Leg was eager to begin the tanning, but had none of the necessary tools, except the knife given to her by her husband. But Glittering Spring and other women of the band gladly lent her everything she needed.

"Your son, Turn Around Walk, is so beautiful," said Spotted Leg to Glittering Spring, as they began tanning the hides.

"For my husband's sake, I hope that our first-born will be a boy."

Turn Around Walk had been born the previous spring. The infant was now walking and trying, with little success, to mimic his parents in speech.

"I have heard your husband talk about it, and I believe he would be happy with any baby, boy or girl," replied Glittering Spring.

Half-jokingly, Spotted Leg said, "If I have a girl, I would want her someday to marry your son."

As the two new friends chatted happily along with other women of the band, they worked without pause on the hides. The flesh side was first prepared by scraping it. Attached to the elk-horn handle was an iron blade, about half the width of a hand, with sharpened fine teeth. With the hide on the ground, the woman stooped and scraped until the hide was the proper thickness. This was a difficult and laborious task, but a good worker could complete four halves or two complete hides in a day.

If a hide was to be made into a robe, the hair was left on. After the hide had been scraped, boiled brains from the buffalo were rubbed into the flesh side, and it was soaked in water overnight. The next day the hide was washed with clean water, then scraped clean until it was white. It was then hung near a fire and hand-rubbed until dry. When dry, the holes along the edges were cut off, and the two halves stitched together with an awl and sinew to form a soft, warm, durable robe.

A hide to be used for a lodge had been kept in one piece when removed from the buffalo. The hair was scraped off, and the skin tanned. The large skins could then be sewn together to make a lodge covering. The number needed ranged from six to as many as eighteen skins. This made a comfortable dwelling that could be taken down and moved from site to site, as the Nakota followed the herds of buffalo through the seasons.

With all the women working and talking together, the work went fast. After several days, Spotted Leg had the skins of all eight buffalo killed by Rides With Broken Leg tanned and sewn into a new lodge covering. Glittering Spring gave her two more skins which they made into robes for sleeping.

Chapter 16

Admiring the lodge after they had erected it with borrowed lodge poles, Glittering Spring said, "Your husband will be proud of your work."

It had been a warm day for the middle of *Wicogandu*, the Center Moon (January), when, nearly without warning, the blizzard struck. Rides With Broken Leg and Gray Horn were hunting pronghorn antelope north of the Missouri River valley when they saw the the black clouds moving toward them from the northwest. As they watched, the clouds turned white near the ground. They knew they had little time.* Abandoning the half-butchered antelope, they immediately struck out for their camp.

The pair arrived shortly before dark, just as the storm hit. Working quickly with cold-numbed fingers, they unloaded the horses and secured them in the rope corral. By the time they made it to their lodges, they could barely see an arm's length in front of them.

The frigid northwest wind howled through the small

. . . .

* Winter storms in this area of Montana can strike with little warning. Temperatures can drop sixty degrees in an hour, and winds can reach over fifty miles per hour as a fast-moving Arctic cold front passes through.

encampment. The twelve lodges were located among the trees along the Missouri River bottom, a short distance downstream from the confluence of the Milk River. The trees provided some protection from the fierce wind and, equally as important, wood for the fires.

When the bands separated for the winter, each group was made up mostly of family members. Rides and his wife had been living with the band of the Paddlers of the Prairie since the previous spring. They had no relatives in the band, and were invited to spend the winter with the families of Glittering Spring and Gray Horn.

"My husband, I am so happy you are back. I was beginning to worry because of the storm. Come sit by the fire. I have made some juneberry tea for you."

Rides removed his jacket, from which the snow was already beginning to melt, and smiled at his wife. "You are more beautiful now than ever. I think it is because of the child you are carrying." He put his arms around her and gently hugged her.

"You can hug me more than that. It will not hurt the baby." She squeezed him tightly. "I love you, husband."

The fire was bright and the lodge warm. Rides sat on a buffalo robe and leaned against the backrest made for him by his wife. He sipped the juneberry tea and watched as Spotted Leg prepared a soup made from bull berries and dried buffalo meat. She first boiled the meat until it was tender, then removed it from the pot and added several handfuls of dried orange-colored bull berries. She hung the pot over the fire and brought it to a boil, then moved it to the side of the fire to simmer. In a short while, Spotted Leg handed her husband a cup of the delicious soup. He savored the combined flavors of buffalo broth and the slightly tart bull berries. It seemed to warm his entire body.

"It is delicious, my dear wife." He looked into her eyes. "In the spring, after the baby is born, we will travel to the Medicine Lodge Dance of my band. I am sure your band will also be there."

"My father will be very angry. He may not want me as his daughter now that I have gone against his will. But I do very much want to see my mother and grandmother. Also, I want to see Blue Calf and thank her for what she has done."

The couple ate the boiled buffalo meat and drank the soup and listened to the fury of the storm. They talked more about the trip to visit their parents and about their baby to be born in early spring. Spotted Leg built up the fire. They removed their clothes and slid beneath a large warm buffalo robe for the night. In a few moments the storm had been forgotten.

By late afternoon of the next day, the storm had passed and the sun again showed itself. However, the wind was still quite strong.

"I am going to speak to Gray Horn. I believe that tomorrow would be a good time to hunt antelope. We can run them into the deep snowdrifts and easily kill them," said Rides.

"Yes, husband. It will be nice to have some fresh antelope meat. We have been eating dried buffalo meat for many days."

The next day, before the sun had reached its high point, eight hunters moved their horses north of the river valley at a trot. The wind had blown nearly all of the snow into deep drifts in the dry stream valleys, leaving the flat areas nearly without snow. The strong winds and blowing snow had left last year's grass lying nearly flat on the ground. The wind had subsided, and all that remained of the former gale was a biting breeze from the northeast. Clouds of steam came from the nostrils of the horses and men.

The hunters had not gone far north before a group of seven antelope were spotted. Gray Horn instructed Rides With Broken Leg and two others, one who had a rifle, to slowly move west and then north to get around the animals. Two others, each with rifles, were to move to the west of the antelope. The others remained with Gray Horn, who also had a rifle. All were to await the signal of Gray Horn, then begin to fire.

The pronghorn antelope have the keenest eyesight of any animal on the plains and are also the most fleet of foot. They run so fast that a horse is like a tortoise in comparison. As a pronghorn flees from danger, its entire rear end, as it bounces across the prairie, looks like a large white flag waving at an enemy.

With their sharp eyes, the animals watched every move made by the humans. Some skittered around, but at this distance of more than five hundred paces, none seemed to be afraid. If the hunters came nearer, the antelope were prepared to spring away and easily could outdistance them.

Once the hunters were all in place, Gray Horn gave a hand signal. The men with guns, including himself, fired their single-shot rifles. As the slug from the north hit an antelope in the leg, the entire group darted south. An instant later the shot from Gray Horn, which missed its mark and slammed into the ground in front of the racing animals, turned them toward the east. The two shots from the west, one of which killed an animal, kept the small herd running east.

The horsemen charged after the antelope, and the animals

panicked. Eyes on their pursuers, the antelope did not see the small valley ahead. They ran directly into the snowdrift that nearly filled the valley. The crusted snow was almost hard enough to bear the weight of the animals, but their sharp hooves cut through the crust.

The men with guns reloaded, while those with bows pursued the animals. When the hunters reached the antelope, the animals were struggling to free themselves from the snowdrift, which was more than three times the depth of a man's height to the bottom of the gully. It was a simple task to kill the remaining six animals.

Once the antelopes had been retrieved from the snowdrift, Gray Horn said a prayer, thanking each animal for giving its life for the benefit of the hunters and their families.

After the prayer, the animals were loaded onto the horses and carried back to the small camp of a dozen lodges along the Missouri River bottom, where the butchering would take place. That night there would much feasting.

CHAPTER 17

She began crying as soon as her body met the air in the lodge. The midwife held her for Spotted Leg to see. "You have a beautiful daughter. She is very strong and healthy." As she spoke, she handed the baby to Glittering Spring. Picking up a small, very sharp knife, the midwife cut and then tied the umbilical cord.

Glittering Spring, sitting beside the new mother, cleansed the baby's nose and mouth, then washed her with warm water. "She is beautiful, and I know your husband will be very proud of you and the baby." She laid the child face down on Spotted Leg, who covered her and put her to her breast.

Spotted Leg, looking at her daughter, forgot the pain of delivery and smiled as tears ran down her face.

It was the middle of *Wicinstayazan*, Sore Eye Moon (March). Outside, the morning star faded as the sun began to rise. The lodge was warm from a fire tended by Glittering Spring.

Glittering Spring helped Spotted Leg sit up, then put a backrest behind her. She went to the fire, returned with a cup and handed it to the new mother. "Drink this juneberry tea. It will help bring on your milk."

"I am so happy that you are the sponsor of my baby. She will turn out to be beautiful and a good woman, wife, and mother, like you."

The midwife stood up and said to Spotted Leg, "You will be fine. I shall come by later in the day." She had put the umbilical cord in a container and set it beside Spotted Leg. The cord would later be dried and put in a diamond-shaped beaded buckskin bag as a keepsake of the birth of the baby. "I shall speak to your husband and let him know that all is well." She left.

Rides With Broken Leg stepped through the lodge entrance beaming. "Oh, my love ..." then stopped when he saw Glittering Spring.

"I must leave now. My husband will be glad to know that the baby is healthy and you are well." Glittering Spring stepped through the lodge entrance and was gone.

"Come, my love, sit beside me and see your daughter. She is beautiful and reminds me of you." She took the baby from her breast and held her for Rides to see. The baby made a squeaking cry. "See, she likes you."

"She is so pink. Is she alright?"

"Yes, she is fine. The midwife said that she is very healthy."

"She has so much hair. I did not know that babies were born with so much hair. Look at her feet and hands. They are so small."

Spotted Leg smiling said, "I see that you like her."

"I love her as I love you. Can I hold her soon?"

Spotted Leg handed the baby to her husband. He looked at her and smiled as he fought back tears. The baby again began a squeaky cry.

Rides handed her back and she was put on the breast. Spotted Leg held the child's head over her breast, and the little girl began sucking enthusiastically.

"Your grandmother and parents will be so proud of you and our daughter."

"I do not think that my parents will ever want to see me again, nor will they want to see our child. My grandmother ... I know she would be happy for us and the baby." Spotted Leg could not hold back the tears.

Rides put his arm around her, "I am sorry. I did not want to make you sad." He held her with one arm and put the fingers of the other hand on the head of his daughter. "I love you both."

They sat for some time. Then Rides said, "When the time comes, we will travel to my band for the Medicine Lodge Dance. I will never forget two years ago when I first saw you after the dance. I thought that you were a vision. Then, for me, you became a vision come true."

"I want to see my grandmother and parents. But I am afraid of my father."

"Do not worry. Once he puts his eyes on the baby, he will not be angry anymore."

In a short time the baby was asleep. Rides removed the backrest so his wife could lie down, and soon she was also asleep. He put more wood on the fire and lay down beside his family.

The baby was first to awaken. Her squeaky cry woke the parents. She was hungry again. Rides put more wood on the fire. A short time later, Glittering Spring, from outside the lodge, asked, "May I come in? I brought some hot soup and meat."

"Where is your son, Turn Around Walk?" asked Spotted Leg. "I think he would like to see the baby. Some day, I know that they will marry." They laughed.

"He is with his father. He can see the baby later when you

are more rested."

After drinking some soup, Rides excused himself. He would take his horses to water, and see if there was enough grass where they were picketed.

Wedu (Spring) passed rapidly, and the new baby seemed to grow every day. It was nearly the middle of *Waheqosmewi*, Full Leaf Moon (June), when the young couple and baby prepared to leave for the Little Rock Mountain Band and the Medicine Lodge Dance. They had heard from a man who had recently returned from visiting relatives that the Medicine Lodge Dance would be held on the northwest side of the Little Rocky Mountains.

Early in the morning, Spotted Leg, with the help of Glittering Spring, took down the lodge and packed their possessions. Rides With Broken Leg brought their three horses. One was harnessed with the travois, on which their belongings were then loaded.

While they worked, Turn Around Walk, now two years old, knelt beside the beaded sleeping bag of the baby and babbled to the little girl. "He likes her very much. I hope our next child will be a girl, too," said Glittering Spring. With tears in her eyes she looked at her friend. "I wish you did not have to go. I will miss you very much. Turn Around Walk will be lost without seeing your baby."

Spotted Leg embraced her. "I will think every day of you and your husband – and all the help and friendship you have given us." She mounted her horse. Glittering Spring handed up the bag in which the baby lay. Turn Around Walk protested, and his mother picked the small boy up and gave him a hug as Spotted Leg, baby on her back, led the horse loaded with their belongings and rode slowly toward the southwest.

Rides With Broken Leg finished saying farewell to his friends, then mounted his buffalo horse and rode after his wife. Not long after they left, three young men decided that they would also like to visit the Little Rock Mountain Band. They raced after Rides, who was glad to have them on the journey with his family.

Seven days later the small group arrived on the north side of the Little Rocky Mountains.

CHAPTER 18

It seemed only a short time since they had left the Paddlers of the Prairie Band. Spotted Leg could still see Glittering Spring, holding her two-year-old, Turn Around Walk, waving at her as Spotted Leg rode away. The baby girl who had been on Spotted Leg's back at that moment was now twelve winters in age. She had been named Courage Walks. Three years after she was born, a son, Standing Cloud, was born.

Time had flown by. Spotted Leg was cutting meat for drying. Her daughter was with her paternal grandmother, Wind Walker. Grandfather Stands Alone was teaching young Standing Cloud how to make a bow. As she carefully sliced the buffalo meat into thin strips, nostalgia overcame Spotted Leg as she remembered the spring when she and her husband had arrived with their baby girl at the village of the Little Rock Mountain Band.

It had been the day after the summer equinox. The medicine man in charge of the Medicine Lodge Dance had instructed the camp crier to announce that the event, the most holy of dances, would begin at the next full moon. The returning couple and their new baby had been welcomed with a feast given by Stands Alone and Wind Walker, parents of Rides With Broken Leg. Old Fire, one of Rides' adopted grandmothers, had also helped in the feast. His other adopted grandmother, Blue Knife Woman, had died during the past winter.

Five days before the moon was full, the Missouri River Dog Band arrived at the village. They had again been invited to participate in the Medicine Lodge Dance. Spotted Leg was happy, but yet afraid to see her parents. Her father might still be very angry at her for eloping.

When the band arrived she put the baby, who had not yet been given a name, on her back and searched for her mother. She found her setting up their lodge. Spotted Leg came up to stand several paces behind her mother and very tentatively said, "Mother."

The woman, startled, whirled around, nearly falling down. "My child! My daughter! We thought that you were dead." With tears in her eyes she ran the few steps and embraced Spotted Leg. She had not realized that her daughter was carrying a baby until she put her arms around her. "What is this? Let me see the child."

"This is your granddaughter. You will love her, she is so beautiful."

The grandmother took the child and held her. With a small voice, Spotted Leg asked the question she almost dared not speak. "Is father still very angry with me for not marrying the man he had chosen?"

"He was angry for some time. Then he was afraid that Black Cliff had killed you and Rides With Broken Leg. He said it was his fault because he had insisted you marry the man against your will. He will be happy to see you, and his grandchild." She asked what had happened to Black Cliff, and Spotted Leg told her the story.

Spotted Leg also learned what had happened to her friend, Blue Calf, who had gone to the marriage ceremony in her place. The day following the interrupted marriage ceremony, Blue Calf had told the whole story to Buffalo Capture. Her mouth and nose were still red and swollen. Buffalo Capture and Blue Calf had talked for most of the day. Buffalo Capture admired her bravery and loyalty to her friend. Six months later, after Buffalo Capture made the proper gifts to her father, the two were married. They were still living with the Missouri River Dog Band and had arrived with the other visitors to celebrate the Medicine Lodge Dance. Blue Calf was expecting a child.

Spotted Leg recalled her reunion with Blue Calf that same day. She held her baby girl and said with joy, "Look what you have done for me. My husband and I are so happy. We have this child ... all because of your courage."

The day following the arrival of the Missouri River Dog Band, Hawk Woman, the mother of Spotted Leg, and Wind Walker gave a feast for the baby girl. The father of Spotted Leg, who was an elder in his band, was asked by his daughter to name the baby. He had heard the story of the courage and bravery of Blue Calf when she went to the marriage ceremony at Black Cliff's lodge and took the place of Spotted Leg. Proudly he held his granddaughter for all to see. In honor of Blue Calf, he named the child Courage Walks. He then gave the baby girl to Blue Calf, who carried the child to Spotted Leg.

That was many years ago. Absorbed in memories, Spotted Leg continued to cut the buffalo meat, but for an unknown reason, her thoughts kept returning to the year that she and her husband had lived with the Paddlers of the Prairie Band. How were their friends Glittering Spring and Gray Horn, and their son Turn Around Walk, she wondered. She wanted to see them again.

She knew that Rides With Broken Leg also had missed that close bond of friendship. Maybe they should visit the Paddlers of the Prairie Band. It would be good to see their friends again. She would talk with her husband about it that evening after the evening meal.

Rides With Broken Leg adjusted his backrest to a lower position and leaned against it, relaxing after the meal of boiled buffalo meat and turnips. Their nine-year-old son, Standing Cloud, had just left to play with friends. The boys were going to practice shooting arrows. Courage Walks had gone to visit her grandmother Wind Walker.

"My love, for the last several days I have been thinking of Glittering Spring and Gray Horn, and the year we spent in their band. That was a good year. Remember, we were just married. Oh, the fun we had." She smiled as she thought back to that time long ago.

Rides remembered also. "Yes, I have thought of that year many times. It *was* a good year. Our daughter was born there. I also miss seeing Gray Horn, and talking and hunting with him. Yes! It was a great year. I hope that some day we can again see them and their baby. I forget, the baby must now be nearly grown. I think that we should go visit them and the Paddlers of the Prairie during this summer. It would be good."

They looked at each other for a long moment. Overcome with emotion, Spotted Leg moved to the side of her husband, knelt down, and put her lips on his cheek. He put his arms around her, holding her close.

A week later, the family set off for the Paddlers of the Prairie Band, which they had heard was now located about one day's ride north of the confluence of the Missouri and Milk rivers. Rides estimated that the journey would take seven days. His father Stands Alone had questioned the wisdom of the four members of the family traveling alone for seven days, because of the danger of being attacked by a war party or raiding party of another tribe. Rides With Broken Leg assured his father that he knew the area well, and the chances of seeing anyone along the way or being attacked were very unlikely. They would come back before the first snow.

They could see the Bear Paw Mountains, about one day's journey by horse, to the south when their journey began. The plan of Rides With Broken Leg was to travel south to the Milk River valley, follow the valley to its confluence with the Missouri, then head northeast. They would soon find signs of the Paddlers band and shortly thereafter be with their friends.

They followed the Milk River valley for the first day of travel. It was near the end of *Wasasa*, Red Berries Moon (July), and the mosquitoes in the valley swarmed over them and the horses. These pests did not bother the dogs because of their fur, but the horses and humans were tormented by the many bites.

Even though game in the valley was plentiful and easy to take, Rides decided that this was not the best travel route. They swung north, leaving the valley and mosquitoes behind, and continued on their way. Other than the everpresent westerly wind, the only noises they heard were the occasional buzzing sound of a grasshopper, and songs of the meadowlarks.

For the journey they had taken five horses and two dogs.

The children rode together on one horse. The parents each rode one horse and led a second horse with a travois which carried their belongings and supplies. They ate their meals from those provisions, mostly dried meat and pemmican. As the first evening fell, Rides found a good place to camp. The night was cool and dry, so they did not set up the lodge. They slept under the stars wrapped in buffalo robes.

During the second day of their journey, Rides killed three sagegrouse. That evening they made camp by a stream, along which chokecherry bushes grew. The cherries were beginning to ripen. The two children, Courage Walks and Standing Cloud, picked cherries while Spotted Leg cooked the grouse on a spit over a fire. To the delight of everyone, the birds and fruit made a nice change from the dried buffalo meat.

The wind died as the sun set with crimson streaks far above the horizon. Standing Cloud said, "Father, I like summer. It is warm, and berries taste so good. Why can we not have summer all of the time?"

"My son, the Nakota did not always have a summer. Long ago, they lived far north where it was cold, and there was snow all year. I will tell you the story of how we came to have summer:

A war party went south and was gone for many moons. Upon returning to their village, they went immediately to the lodge of the chief.

They told him that they had been in a land that did not have snow. It was many days' journey in the direction of the midday sun. In the middle of a large village was a yellow lodge in which the summer was kept in a bag, hung from a tripod. It was guarded day and night by four old men – one at the lodge entrance, one at the back of the lodge, and one on each side of the tripod.

The chief had the camp crier call all the councilors together in his lodge. After they all had heard the story, one of the council members said, 'Let us call the representatives of each kind of the fastest running animals and ask them to help us.'

The chief had the camp crier call to his lodge all the medicine men who had fast-running animals as helpers. When all were assembled, the chief said, 'My people, and my brothers (the animals), we have learned that far in the direction of the midday sun is the summer. We ask that you help bring it to us. The ones who go to bring summer back will never return, but a great good would be done for our people and our brothers. Their children will have the warmth of summer forever.'

The council decided to send the Lynx, the Red Fox, the Antelope, the Coyote, and the Wolf. The young warriors who knew the way would guide the runners to the village where summer was held.

After many days of travel they arrived at the village where summer was kept in the yellow lodge. They held a council and decided that the Lynx, who could not be heard when he walked, would be the one to go to the yellow lodge and bring back the bag containing summer.

The other runners were stationed according to

the distance which they could swiftly run.

The Red Fox was stationed first, then the Antelope, the Coyote, and finally the long-winded Wolf. The young warriors waited across a frozen river to the north, where the runners were to bring the bag containing summer.

Early the next morning, before there was yet light, while sleep was heavy in every lodge, the Lynx crept to the entrance and peered into the yellow lodge. The four old men slept soundly.

Summer, in the form of spring water, was hanging from the tripod in the back of the lodge. It moved back and forth in the bag, made from the stomach of a buffalo, and now and then, some of it trickled from the bag onto the ground beneath the tripod. From it sprang forth green grass, flowers, and many other beautiful plants.

"Were berries growing there also, father?" asked Standing Cloud.

"Yes, son, berries were growing there. Now, to continue ...

The Lynx silently entered the lodge, and snapped the cord that held the bag containing summer. Seizing it in his teeth, he sprang out of the lodge. The guards awakened, saw that summer had been taken by the Lynx, and alerted the village. Warriors on fast horses pursued the Lynx.

The Lynx carried the bag containing summer to the Red Fox, who took it and ran to the north. As the Fox ran toward the next station, the warriors from the south caught and killed the Lynx. The warriors nearly caught the Fox before he could give the summer to the Antelope. The Fox, too, was killed by the warriors.

The Antelope carried the summer to the Coyote. The Antelope was then caught and killed by the warriors.

The fast horses of the warriors were nearly upon the Coyote when he gave the bag to the long-winded Wolf. The Coyote ran off, but also was caught and killed.

As the Wolf ran to the north, all the snow through which he passed melted. Green grass and flowers sprang forth. The warriors were nearly upon him when he reached the frozen river.

As he carried the summer across, the ice behind him melted and broke up. When the warriors from the south reached the river, it was running full with ice, leaving them stranded.

The warriors from the south stopped at the river's edge and spoke in sign language to the Nakota. They said, 'Let us bargain about who has possession of summer.'

After some time, it was agreed that each could have summer for six moons. At the end of the six moons, summer would be carried back to the river and delivered to the waiting party.

After that, for a while, we had two seasons: the *Waniyedu* (winter), and the *Mnogedu* (summer).

"Why did the animal runners have to die, father?" asked Standing Cloud.

"Son, the chief of the Nakota told that it would be so. They sacrificed their lives for the Nakota and the animals so that all may have summer."

Rides continued:

> After many years with two seasons, the Nakota council decided that they would have the cranes carry the summer back and forth. The cranes were the first migratory birds to go south. They moved south in stages. When they found good feeding grounds, they stayed for long periods.
>
> In this way the winter came on slowly, rather than quickly as it had when the summer was carried by the young warriors. This was the way the *Pdanyedu* (fall) season made its appearance.
>
> When the cranes made their way north again, the snow melted and there were signs in both plants and animals that summer was on the way. That time of the year was called the *Wedu* (spring) season.
>
> When fall or spring arrived late, it was a sign that the cranes had tarried a long time along the way. An early fall or spring indicated that the cranes winged their way south or north in haste.
>
> The cranes always circled and called loudly, as they flew over a village, to announce their arrival or departure.

That is how the Nakota came to have four seasons: the *Waniyedu* (winter), the *Mnogedu* (summer), the *Pdanyedu* (fall), and *Wedu* (spring).

When Rides With Broken Leg finished the story, the western sky was darkening, but crimson and purple rays could still be seen. The evening star had risen in the east.

"Father, I am very happy that the Nakota found summer. I would not like to live in the snow all the time. I like winter sometimes, but the summer is still the best," said Standing Cloud.

On the sixth day of their journey, they reached Porcupine Creek. They were about a half-day's ride north of the confluence of the Missouri and Milk rivers and in the vicinity of the last reported location of the Paddlers of the Prairie.

Rides With Broken Leg made the decision to camp for the night, since there was plenty of water and grass for the horses. During the remainder of the afternoon, he and nine-year-old Standing Cloud would search for sign of the Paddlers of the Prairie. While they were gone, Spotted Leg and Courage Walks would set up camp and prepare the evening meal.

Father and son rode only a short distance to the north along the stream when they spotted an area where there had been a large encampment of at least one hundred lodges only a short while ago. Rides With Broken Leg studied the area closely and determined that it had been the Paddlers of the Prairie band. The trail indicated that they had moved to the north within the last two days. Tomorrow his family would overtake and join the band. Rides and his son returned to their camp with the good news.

Excited at the news, Courage Walks suggested that they continue their trek. They still had plenty of daylight and could possibly find the band before dark. Her father agreed they might be able to find the band – however, they were in a nice area and it would be good to rest and have a hot evening meal. They would leave at daybreak on the next morning.

After the family finished their meal, Courage Walks went to the stream to wash the cooking pots. The sun was sinking in the west as she thought excitedly about tomorrow. Her mother had told her so much about her sponsor, Glittering Spring, and about Glittering Spring's son, Turn Around Walk.

As she was about to leave the stream, the pounding of hooves could be heard. Her first thought was that their horses, which had been picketed, had been frightened and ran off. Then she heard the war cries coming from the direction of the setting sun.

Courage Walks moved to a point where the camp could be seen through the willows. It was about fifty paces to the west of the stream. Eight horseman, riding at full speed, charged the camp.

The girl tried to scream a warning to her parents to run, but no sound came from her mouth. She saw her father grab his rifle which, along with his lance, leaned against a tripod. He shot and killed the lead rider. By that time, the others were nearly upon him.

Rides With Broken Leg swung the heavy rifle and knocked another warrior from his horse. He threw down the rifle and grabbed his lance. Running backwards, he tried to retreat toward his wife and son. A bullet hit him in the left shoulder knocking him on his back. He quickly arose and threw the lance at the attacker. The man screamed as the lance blade went completely through his thigh and into the ribs of his horse, pinning him to the animal. The horse screamed and began lunging and bucking, throwing the warrior to the ground. As the man fell, the lance was pulled from the ribs of the horse, at the same time cutting completely through the thigh muscle of the warrior.

The warrior who had been knocked from his horse by the blow from Rides' rifle had recovered enough to rise to his knees. While Rides was fighting to keep off the other attackers, the man retrieved his rifle, took careful aim, and shot Rides With Broken Leg through the heart.

Before the attack, Standing Cloud had been practicing with the bow and arrows made for him by his grandfather, Stands Alone. He took aim at the man who had shot his father and let fly an arrow. The toy arrow hit the man in the right eye. The man groaned, covered his face, and fell backwards. As the man fell, another warrior swung his war club, which hit the boy in the back of the skull, killing him instantly.

Spotted Leg lunged at the man who had killed her son and stabbed him in the hip with the knife which she used to butcher buffalo. She pulled the knife out to make another thrust when the war club smashed into her skull. She too fell, never to rise again.

The shock of the slaughter of her parents and brother was too great for Courage Walks, and she was unable to move. Stunned, she watched the attackers for a short while, and heard them speak as they tended their wounded. It was a language which she did not understand. Then one of the men came directly at her, and she thought that he had seen her. Fear and the need to escape overcame her immobility. She must run and hide before the man reached her. If not, he would find and kill her.

Courage Walks crouched down behind the streambank and ran along the edge of the water, through the gravel where her footprints would not show. She hid in a large clump of willows. From this vantage point, she watched as the man came through the willows and stood at the edge of the stream. He looked both upstream and downstream, then squatted down and filled a water bag. She realized that he had not seen her. He had come to the stream for water to wash the wounds of his companions.

Courage Walks could hear the warriors speaking in their strange language. Were they Crows? Her father had spoken many times of the Crow and their ability to steal horses. However, the five horses which they would take back came at a great cost, both to them and to the Nakota family.

Courage Walks remained in her hiding place until the twilight had nearly faded into darkness, listening to the occasional groans from one of the wounded. When it was dark enough, she slipped from the willows, crouching low, and moved swiftly downstream, making sure to stay on the gravel near the edge of the stream.

She traveled along the flat gravel bottoms of Porcupine Creek until she could barely see in the darkness. She crossed the stream and proceeded along the east bank, until, exhausted, she lay down behind a large clump of sagebrush and wept silently as the horror of the slaughter of her family raced through her mind.

The sun was above the horizon when Courage Walks opened her tear-stained eyes. She was awakened by the sound of horses and men speaking. She curled up beneath the sagebrush and froze, trying not breath. She could hear her heart beating as she peaked around the sage.

Across the stream, Courage Walks could see the attackers. They had taken the five horses that belonged to her family. One horse carried the dead warrior. Two other horses pulled travois – one carried the man wounded in the thigh by her father, and the other bore the man wounded in the hip by her mother. The man who had been shot in the eye by her brother followed behind, with a covering over his blinded right eye. They were moving south toward the Missouri River.

Courage Walks waited until the party was out of sight. Then she crossed the stream, not even feeling the cold water, and returned to the camp. She gasped when she saw the bodies of her father, mother, and brother. They lay in rigid, completely unnatural forms where they had been killed. She wished that she could wrap and raise the bodies high into a tree. But all that she could do was cover the bodies with buffalo robes.

The attackers had eaten or taken most of their food. She did find some dried buffalo meat in a buckskin bag. She also located a water bag, which she filled.

Courage Walks began to leave, then turned and walked back to where her mother had been slain. The twelve-year-old girl picked up the bloodied knife her mother had used to slash her murderer.

She would go north. Her father said that he had seen signs of the Paddlers of the Prairie Band not far from their camp.

She would follow the trail and find the band. She would get help to take proper care of the bodies of her loved ones. Tears ran down her face, but she could not turn and look back as she left the camp.

Courage Walks followed the Porcupine Creek valley north until about midday, when she stopped to eat some of the dried meat and drink from the stream. After resting for a short while, she turned east and walked out of the valley. Before the sun had set, she crossed the path taken by the Paddlers of the Prairie. The grass had been beaten down by several hundred people, horses, and dogs. She turned north and followed their path.

As she walked, the girl never saw the beauty of the sunset, as orange and lavender rays shot high into the western sky. She never noticed that the breeze, everpresent during the day, had stopped. Nor did she notice the stillness and quiet that came over the land. The bird songs, grasshopper buzzing, and all other sound had ceased. Her mind was filled with sorrow and anger. She must find the band soon, so she could get help to take care of the bodies of her parents.

Courage Walks continued to move slowly northward until she could no longer see the trail in the darkness. She sat down exhausted and sobbed. Later she tried but could not bring herself to eat. She lay down on the prairie and looked up at the stars, though her eyes did not see them. As she listened to the howl of a lone wolf, she wished she had died along with her family.

Early the next morning she awoke shivering. She must move on. She chewed on some dried meat as she trudged northward. Would she ever find the friends of her parents?

In the early afternoon of the third day, Courage Walks sat

down in the trampled grass and wondered how long she could continue. Her food was gone and there was only a small amount of water remaining. She wanted to be dead. Exhausted, she lay down in a prone position and slept.

In the late afternoon, the young girl awoke and again began to move north along the path taken by the Paddlers of the Prairie. The soles of her moccasins had worn through, and she limped as she walked. It was a hot day. She took a sip of the last of the water, and continued walking.

Suddenly she heard the sound of running horses. She turned and saw several riders coming from the west. Had the killers of her parents found her? She thought that she had escaped them. Could they have followed her tracks?

Courage Walks wanted to hide, but the prairie provided no where to hide except in the tall grass. She crouched down, but it was too late. They had seen her. She took out her mother's large butchering knife and stood straight up in defiance. She would fight.

The lead horseman came to a halt a few paces from her and dismounted. She held the knife pointed toward him. Her hair had not been combed, nor had her face and hands been washed since the day her parents died, and her clothing was soiled from sleeping on the ground.

The man said, "My child, are you all right? Have you been hurt?"

Courage Walks understood the words! These were not the killers of her parents; these were Nakota. She dropped the knife and fell to the ground, sobbing.

Gray Horn came and knelt beside the girl. He picked her off the ground and held her in his arms. After she stopped crying, one of other warriors brought water. Gray Horn let her drink, then gently washed her hands and face. As they sat, he gave her a piece of pemmican which she hungrily ate. By this time she had become calm. "Where are your parents?" he asked.

Courage Walks told the story of the attack, and of the death of her family. She told about her parents' plans to travel to the Paddlers of the Prairie band, to visit their friends Gray Horn and her sponsor Glittering Spring. Now all she wanted was to go back to her grandparents.

Gray Horn told her who he was, and that she would live with his family until she could be returned to her grandparents. He lifted her up and sat her on his horse, then mounted behind her.

Courage Walks said, "My knife! My knife! I must have it. It is mother's knife."

One of the warriors picked up the long-bladed butchering knife and gave it to her. Together, they rode back to the village of the Paddlers of the Prairie.

When they arrived and dismounted, Glittering Spring ran up to Courage Walks, and with tears in her eyes, hugged her. "My child, you are beautiful. You are the image of your mother. I would have known you anywhere."

The young girl began to sob. Her sponsor stroked her hair and held her tight until the weeping stopped. After Courage Walks had eaten some pemmican and drank tea, Glittering Spring asked, "Do you want to talk about what happened with your parents and brother?" Courage Walks shook her head, and again began to sob.

Glittering Spring again held the girl until the crying subsided. "Come, my child, we will go to the stream, and you can bathe. I will get some new clothes for you."

Not long after, Courage Walks, clothed in a new dress, relaxed for the first time in many days as Glittering Spring combed her long, black, sparkling hair. "You are the image of your mother, but you have the smile of your father," said Glittering Spring.

"I miss my mother, my father, and my brother." Tears again came to the girl's eyes.

"I understand, my child. Now that they are gone, I will be your mother. You will be my daughter, the one that I always wanted but could never have." She hugged Courage Walks.

Fourteen-year-old Turn Around Walk burst through the lodge entrance, "Mother! Mother! I just heard –" He stared at the young girl whose hair was being combed by his mother.

"This is Courage Walks, my son. She will be staying with us for some time. You may not remember her. You were two years old when she, as a baby, and her parents left our village and went to the band of the Little Rock Mountain People."

Courage Walks stood up. She was nearly as tall as Turn Around Walk. She smiled shyly at the boy, who blushed.

The following day, Glittering Spring rode beside Courage Walks as the young girl led Gray Horn and four other men south to the camp on Porcupine Creek where her family had met death. Gray Horn and the other men wrapped the bodies, which had been partially eaten by coyotes and magpies, in un tanned buffalo hides. They then hoisted up the bodies up into the branches of a cottonwood tree.

When the bodies were lashed in place, Gray Horn prayed to Wahkonda and the guardian spirit of Rides With Broken Leg that revenge would be taken against the enemy who had committed this act. He prayed that the spirits of the dead loved ones be protected.

With tears in her eyes, Courage Walks felt a little better in her sorrow, now that the bodies of her family were taken care of properly.

CHAPTER 19

Courage Walks looked up from making pemmican and saw Turn Around Walk staring at her. She smiled at the boy and continued to shape the tasty pemmican patties, made from buffalo meat, cherries, and a little rendered tallow.

It had been nearly two moons since her family had been killed. Frost was on the ground nearly every morning, and the winds from the north had the feel of winter. The cranes carrying summer were on their way south. The Paddlers of the Prairie Band was preparing to move from its location near Old Wives Lake (near current-day Moose Jaw, Saskatchewan) to the Missouri River valley for the winter. They would split up into family groups of eight to twelve lodges for the winter.

Gray Horn and Glittering Spring had taken care of the girl as their own daughter. However, they had promised to return Courage Walks to the band of her parents. There, she would live with her grandparents, Stands Alone and Wind Walker.

When the band broke camp near the end of *Wahpegiwi,* Yellow Leaf Moon (September), Gray Horn and his family, along with Courage Walks, and four young warriors moved southwest in the direction of the last known location of the Little Rock Mountain Band.

Courage Walks was anxious to return to her grandparents,

but thought it would be impossible to tell them of the death of her family. No! She did not want to go back to the Little Rock Mountain Band. Tears came to her eyes. Her mind was in turmoil. Why did her family have to die? It was the fault of her father. He should have followed the advice of grandfather Stands Alone and not gone on the journey. No, it was her mother's fault. She was the one who wanted to visit the Paddlers of the Prairie Band in the first place. I hate them both, she thought. Sobbing, she said aloud, "I love them."

"My child, what is it?" Glittering Spring put her arms around the girl and held her until the crying subsided.

"It hurts so much. Why? Why did they have to die? Will the pain ever go away? At times I am so angry at them for getting killed."

"No, my child, the pain will never completely leave. You will get over your anger, and in time the pain will not be as sharp as it is now. Try to think of the good things about your parents and that will help the pain. I remember them – how they loved each other and how they loved you. They would want you to be strong and carry on their love through your life."

"Mother told me about when she and father eloped. I remember the story of Blue Calf when she stood in for mother at the wedding." Nearly laughing, Courage Walks said, "I have always liked that story. Now, I have met Blue Calf and her family. I am so proud to be named for her."

"What else do you remember about your parents?"

"I remember father saying that life can be hard, but if we have courage, it can be fun. He also said that his guardian spirit would always protect me."

"Remember those things when you become sad."

"I will. But I still miss them and my brother." With hands over her heart, she said, "The pain is still here." She began to cry quietly. Glittering Spring held the child in her arms until the tears stopped.

A light snow was falling when the small party of Gray Horn arrived in the late afternoon at the village of the Little Rock Mountain Band. They were met by two soldiers, who led them to the lodge of Stands Alone and Wind Walker. On the way to the lodge, the soldiers said that the visitors were very fortunate to have arrived on this day, because the next day the band would disperse for the winter.

When they came in view of the lodge, Courage Walks leapt from the horse she was riding and ran ahead of the group. "Grandmother! Grandfather!" she shouted as she dashed toward the lodge. She was nearly to the lodge entrance when Stands Alone stepped out. The girl could not stop, and crashed into her grandfather, nearly knocking him to the ground.

He had barely recovered when Wind Walker stepped from the entrance.

"My granddaughter, you are back," said Wind Walker, hugging the girl. Looking at the strangers sitting on their horses nearby, she asked, "Where are your parents and brother?"

Courage Walks burst into tears.

Gray Horn and his family dismounted. Turn Around Walk held the reins of the horses as his parents introduced themselves to the grandparents of Courage Walks. Gray Horn explained that Rides With Broken Leg, his wife Spotted Leg, and their son had been killed by a Crow war party. Stands Alone stared in disbelief, as Wind Walker held her sobbing granddaughter.

The wind whipped up, and the snowfall began to increase. Stands Alone said, "Come into our lodge where you will be our guests." The soldiers invited the four young warriors who had accompanied Gray Horn's family to stay at the guest lodge.

The wind died during the night, and the snowfall had stopped by sunrise. The day was warm. The entire band split into family units, packed their lodges and belongings, and separated toward their chosen winter campgrounds.

As usual, Stands Alone, with some relatives and friends, moved to the east slope of the Little Rocky Mountains. It was early afternoon when they set up winter headquarters near a large warm spring that flowed from the base of the mountain. Elk and deer were plentiful in this area and would sustain the camp during the winter.

Gray Horn and his family accompanied the group to the camp. They liked the area, and at the invitation of Stands Alone, they decided to remain. In all there were twelve lodges.

Turn Around Walk was happy with the decision to remain. It was very warm on the day they arrived, and he, along with three other boys about his age, went for a swim in the large pool formed by the warm waters from the spring. They disrobed in the brush near the spring, then jumped into the pool, leaving their clothes hanging in the brush.

While the boys were yelling and splashing water on each other, five girls about their age, including Courage Walks, arrived. They began taunting the boys and telling them to come out of the water. The boys stopped playing and tried to hide under the long grass near the edge of the pool. When the boys did not come out, the girls, laughing, took the clothes hanging in the brush and hid them. The boys yelled for the girls to return their clothes, but to no avail.

Glittering Spring had been busy setting up the lodge. It was nearly sundown when she finished putting each person's belongings in the proper place. She called for Turn Around Walk, but got no response. She went out to search for some firewood. Passing near the spring, she heard the boys talking.

"It is getting cold. We will freeze before we get back to the camp," said one.

"My parents will be very angry if I come home naked," said another.

"Those girls who took our clothes – when I catch them, they will regret what they did," said the first.

"Look, I made a skirt of grass," said Turn Around Walk. With that he jumped out of the pool and ran toward the camp, the grass skirt flapping behind. The other boys scrambled out of the water and ran naked in the twilight to their lodges. Glittering Spring smiled as she watched them go.

"Where have you been all afternoon, my son?" asked Glittering Spring as she entered the lodge carrying an armful of wood.

"I was playing with friends," said her son, as he finished tying the top of his buckskin shirt.

"Your hair is wet."

"That is from the spring. We washed in the pool."

Glittering Spring smiled, "It is nice that you will be clean for the evening meal," she said, as she thought of the girls laughing at the boys.

CHAPTER 20

"Husband, I am happy that you are home from the trading post. Some time, I would like to go inside and see all the things which they have to trade," said Courage Walks, as she stirred the pot of turnip soup over a small fire.

"I do not like to be inside the place. The trader calls it Fort Union.* When you are inside, the high wall makes you feel uneasy because you are so closed in." Turn Around Walk put his arms around himself in a gesture of the feeling. "You cannot even see anything on the outside, unless you climb up nearly to the top of the wall where there is a small pathway."

"Why do they have this high wall?"

"Someone told me that they are afraid that the Nakota, or the Bloods, or some other group will attack them. The wall

. . . .

* Fort Union was built by the American Fur Company in 1828 near the meeting of the Missouri and Yellowstone rivers. In 1805, Lewis and Clark had noted the strategic importance of the location for future trade with the Indians. Surrounded by a 20-foot-high stockade, the fort was situated on the north bank of the Missouri, just west of the confluence of the Yellowstone. Steamboats began servicing Fort Union in 1832. The trading post did a good business with the tribes of the Upper Missouri until the early 1850s, when the trade began to wane. By the mid-1860s, the fort fell into disrepair and was abandoned.

will protect them."

"Why would we want to attack them? They have done nothing to us."

"I know we would not attack them. However, I did see a group of Crow warriors and their families while I was there. I do not trust them. They would certainly attack the trading post and steal everything, if they had the chance." He changed the subject. "Dear wife, next time I go to the trading post, I will trade the hides which you tanned for some cloth. Also, I will buy a new knife for you for butchering."

"Thank you, my love. With the cloth, I will make a shawl for myself, and a cap for Looking Glass Hand. However, I do not need a new knife."

Hearing her name, the twelve-year-old girl came from the back of the lodge and stepped to the lodge entrance. She said, "I am going to visit a friend," and quickly was gone.

"I must also be going. There is a meeting about the next buffalo hunt," said Turn Around Walk. He touched the hand of his wife and left.

Courage Walks thought about a new butchering knife. The knife she now used was the one that had once belonged to her mother. It was the very knife that, many years ago, as a young girl, Courage Walks had removed from the camp on Porcupine Creek the morning after her parents and brother had been killed. Now, the blade was very narrow and thin from countless grindings by the sharpening stone.

The thought of a new knife – and the Crow warriors her husband had just seen at the trading post – caused memories to come flooding back, memories of struggle and death, of nightmares and daytime fears that had lasted for a long time after that tragic event. She tried to put the thoughts out of her mind, but began shaking and had to lie down.

When Turn Around Walk returned from the meeting, he stepped through the lodge entrance, looked at Courage Walks, and said, "My wife, are you ill?"

Courage Walks was now sitting up, her face stained with tears. "The knife and the Crows brought back all the memories of ..." Tears began again.

Turn Around Walk stepped across the lodge and sat beside her. "My love, I am sorry. I should have known not to talk about buying a new knife."

She hugged her husband, who kissed her forehead. "Do not blame yourself. I thought that the memories had gone."

The next day, Turn Around Walk began crafting a new bow from cherry wood. He felt someone watching him and looked up to see his wife. "Why are you smiling?"

"I was just thinking about you, years ago."

"I do not understand. Was it something I said? Something I did?"

"That look in your eye, while working on the bow." Her laughing eyes met his. Courage Walks continued, "It is the same look you had when you found your clothes missing and had to run, water dripping from your grass skirt, from the large warm spring to your lodge."

"I said that you would regret that." His slight frown turned into a grin. "Remember, winter came soon after, and I decided to wait until springtime to get even. But the winter was so cold and long that when the warm weather returned, I had forgotten about the grass skirt."

He laughed. "That must have been nearly twenty years ago."

Courage Walks laughed too. "The large bubbling spring at the base of the mountain never froze because it was so warm. I will never forget the steam that rose from it during the cold weather. It appeared that someone kept a fire going under the spring all the time. Grandmother Wind Walker used to take me and several other girls down to bathe in the warm water even when water in the pots outside our lodge was frozen."

A smile covered the face of Turn Around Walk as his mind pictured the events of that winter. "I remember. That is when I first knew I loved you."

"You should have told me."

"I was only fourteen, and you would have laughed at me and told the other girls. And they would have laughed also."

Courage Walks smiled, "I was twelve years old at that time. The same age as our daughter Looking Glass Hand is now. How things have changed. I have so many memories of those times. It was like yesterday – I was watching the steam come off the great spring when ..." Tears came to her eyes again. "... when grandmother came to me. She said that Grandfather Stands Alone had died."

Turn Around Walk touched the hand of his wife. "Yes, I remember."

"It seemed such a short time since my family had been killed. Then grandfather died. A short while later, you and your parents left for your own band. I thought I would never see you again."

"I knew that I would come back someday and marry you."

Courage Walks sat down beside her husband and took his hand. "The following spring, grandmother Wind Walker also died. I will never forget that day. It was a day before the full moon. The Medicine Lodge Dance was to begin the next day." Her mind raced through the events of that long-ago time. "I could not watch any of the celebration." Tears welled in her eyes. "All I could do was ... cry."

"I understand, my love. I wish I had been there to hold your hand."

"It was fortunate for me that the Missouri River Dog Band was in attendance at the Medicine Lodge ceremonies. My mother's parents took me into their lodge. I do not remember the ceremonies, but I do remember that there was a very large thunderstorm soon after the Medicine Lodge was taken down. Everyone was happy. The Thunderbird had spoken. I knew the coming year would be good for the Nakota. But the past year had not been good for me."

Turn Around Walk hugged his wife. "The things you have said reminded me of when we met again, two years later. Remember? It was the year that the Little Rock Mountain Band, the Missouri River Dog Band, and my band all camped together near the Little Rocky Mountains for the Medicine Lodge Dance. You were not a child any longer, but had grown into a beautiful young woman. I still remember your hair was in one long braid which hung nearly to your waist. You wore a white buckskin dress, and had red paint on your cheeks."

"How can you remember all of that?" She smiled, "All I remember is that when we met I said, 'Hello, Turn Around Walk,' and you stared at me. Then you said, 'Ah, ah ...,' nodded your head, turned and left. I thought you did not like me, or had forgotten me."

"You did not know, but I could not take my eyes off of you. I tried not to let you see me staring at you. Whenever you looked my way, I turned away. I felt so alone when you went back to your lodge. It was not until three days later that I had the courage to speak to you. I had been in a battle with the Piegans three moons earlier, and it took more courage to speak to you than to do battle with them."

Courage Walks squeezed his hand, "I am happy that you did speak to me."

She pressed her full lips to his. "Two years later, we were married. What fun we had."

Looking Glass Hand burst into the lodge. "Mother! Father! One of my friends said that her father heard at the fort that a steamboat will be coming up the river soon. Maybe tomorrow. Can I go with my friend and watch the boat as it comes in?"

"We all should go and see the arrival of this boat," said Courage Walks.

"I think that would be nice, but I will not be able to go with you," said Turn Around Walk. "Early tomorrow morning, I will be going with the other scouts to locate a buffalo herd for our next hunt. At last report, the largest herd was at least two days northwest of our camp here near the fort. We should be back in four or five days."

"Father! Father! Could you not wait for another day so you also could watch the boat?"

"No, my child. Soon we will begin to run low on meat. We also need more hides to trade for cloth and tools here at the fort. The boat may still be here when I return."

As they continued to talk, Courage Walks began to prepare the evening meal. Later she would pack some food for her husband's trip.

CHAPTER 21

Looking Glass Hand jumped through the lodge entrance. "Mother! Mother! The boat is coming. We can see the smoke. Someone said that it will be here this afternoon. Can we go see it come in? Mother, can we go down to the river?"

"Yes, my daughter," said Courage Walks. "We will go watch the boat as it comes to the bank and is tied there."

"Oh mother, I wish father would have stayed to see the boat. I did not want him to leave this morning."

"I know how you feel, but he had to go find food. The entire camp will move within a few days after he and the others return. They will guide us to the buffalo, and we will have fresh meat again."

"When can we go to the river, mother?"

"After we eat our midday meal. I am sewing a hat for you from the cloth your father bought yesterday at the fort. Please start a fire. We will have buffalo and turnip soup."

Mother and daughter had just finished their meal when they heard the whistle announcing the arrival of the steamboat. Looking Glass Hand bounded to the lodge entrance and shouted, "It is here, mother. Let us go down to the river."

Along with most of the encampment, they spent much of the afternoon watching the white men unload trade goods from the boat. They could see the guns, knives and axes, pots and pans, large boxes of cloth and blankets, fire-steel used with flint to start fires, and numerous other items being unloaded. What they could not see was the scourge of the Nakota – something much more deadly than guns and knives.

By that evening, Turn Around Walk and the other three scouts were camped on the banks of the Big Muddy Creek. In late afternoon they had killed five sagegrouse, which were now roasting on a spit over the fire. As they sat watching the birds cooking, they discussed the next day's activities. As night fell, they watched the evening star appear, and a short time later the northern lights began dancing on the horizon.

Turn Around Walk lay back on his robe and watched the infinite beauty of the cloudless night sky, but his thoughts were with his family. He remembered the excitement in the eyes and voice of Looking Glass Hand as she told them the news about the boat. He remembered that his wife seemed disappointed he would not be able to go with them to watch the arrival of the boat.

As he watched the dancing lights to the north, he held his medicine bag and asked his guardian spirit to protect his loved ones. He did not completely trust the people at the fort, with their strange ways and desires – and amazing machines like the noisy steamboat, with its churning paddles and smoke belching into the prairie sky. And all the warriors and their families from different tribes – including the Crow – gathering to watch the spectacle.

The scouts were up before the sun had risen. The early spring morning was cold, and frost could be seen in spots along the valley bottom. The horses, which had been picketed so they could graze, had been taken to the creek for water and now were readied for the day's scouting trip. Turn Around Walk had rebuilt the fire and heated some leftover grouse.

When all had eaten, the scouts rode in a northwesterly direction. After a short while, they decided to separate to cover a larger territory. It was agreed to meet that evening at the southern end of Big Muddy Lake. Turn Around Walk, along with his friend Two Strike, rode in a westerly direction until the sun was about halfway to the zenith. Then they turned north in the direction of the rendezvous point.

Late in the afternoon, the two riders crossed the trail of a large herd of buffalo. "The herd cannot be more than a half-day's ride to the north. The tracks are quite fresh," said Turn Around Walk.

"Yes. From the width of the grazing area, there must be at least two thousand animals." said Two Strike.

They followed the trail which led in the direction of Big Muddy Lake.

They had not traveled far until Two Strike said, "See the dust? We are very near to the herd. It appears they are moving toward the lake." In a short time they reached the tail end of the herd. Taking advantage of the gentle wind coming toward them from the northwest, the scouts rode very close to several grazing cows and calves without the near-sighted animals getting the scent of humans or horses.

Turn Around Walk took his rifle from its beaded buckskin case and in a low voice said, "We need meat for tonight, and for the remainder of the journey." He stepped off his horse, handed the rein to his partner, knelt, aimed, and shot a fat calf. The cows and calves ran off a short distance, looked back at the humans, and sniffed the air. In a short time they were calmly back to grazing, except for the cow which lost her calf. She bellowed, searching for her calf. She moved near the humans, smelled the blood, and immediately turned, still bellowing, to rejoin the herd.

Turn Around Walk moved to the calf, bowed and touched the dead creature on the head, and thanked the spirit of the animal that it had given its life for the needs of the men as was intended by Wahkonda.

The shot had been heard by the other scouts, who soon arrived on the scene to find Turn Around Walk and Two Strike butchering the animal.

That night the scouts camped on the edge of Big Muddy Lake. The large buffalo herd also bedded down for the night near the lake, to the west. Tomorrow the scouts would begin the journey back to Fort Union and their families, but tonight they would enjoy fresh meat and discuss the hunt to come.

The following morning, after packing the buffalo meat, the scouts rode south toward the Missouri River. The day was gray. By the time they reached Big Muddy Creek where they had camped the first night, a steady rain was falling. In a short time the group had built a lean-to of cottonwood branches, covered it with long grass and the hide of the buffalo calf, and took shelter. The horses were watered and picketed while Turn Around Walk struck a fire. They would eat and spend the night in relative comfort – warm, dry, and with full stomachs.

The next morning the rain still fell, and the group decided to wait till it stopped before continuing their journey. All day they rested, talked, ate, and watched the rain, which did not diminish until evening. As the sun set, the scouts could see the red sky and knew the next day would be good for traveling. They would be with their families by the following evening.

On the day after the steamboat arrived, Courage Walks visited her friend Two Star. The husband of Two Star had traded four buffalo skins for calico cloth which had arrived on the steamboat. Two Star spread out the cloth and showed it to her friend. Not knowing that the cloth carried death, Courage Walks held the calico against her cheek and said, "It is beautiful and so soft. After the next buffalo hunt, I will tan enough hides so my husband can also trade for this cloth."

"I plan to make a new dress, and a skirt for my daughter. If enough cloth remains I will make a shirt for my husband," said Two Star. The two women laughed together in happiness.

While the women visited, they heard rain begin to fall on the lodge. "I must go and help Looking Glass Hand. She and a friend went to the river to gather wood. I like the white man's cloth very much – it is so pretty and easy to cut and sew. I know the dress you plan to make will be beautiful." Courage Walks stepped out of the lodge and moved toward the river.

Earlier that morning, the two girls had each taken a dog with a travois to the banks of the river, upstream of the trading post. There they gathered enough wood to last for several days and loaded it on the travois. While the dogs lay on the ground, the girls threw stones into the water to watch them splash. They saw a beaver floating downstream. They laughed as he slapped his tail on the water. Enthralled with the beaver, they hardly noticed the light drizzle when it began to fall. One of the dogs barked, and the beaver dived and disappeared.

Looking Glass Hand looked around. "It is raining, we must go." Quickly they harnessed the dogs to the travois and started back toward the camp.

In the meantime, Courage Walks moved toward the river. As she passed the soldiers' lodge, several men, including the chief of the Paddlers of the Prairie Band, were gathered outside the lodge speaking excitedly. One soldier said, "We must move our camp immediately. We saw the man from the boat. He has red spots on his face and hands. He is now at the fort and may die. It is the evil smallpox."

Another said, "I do not believe that it is a problem for us. Let us wait and see. The buffalo scouts will return soon. We will then move the entire camp to where the buffalo are located."

Courage Walks had never seen anyone who had the dreaded disease, but her grandfather Stands Alone had told her the story of his parents, and her grandmother Wind Walker's parents – how they and many people of their band had died so terribly from the curse.

The news was spreading rapidly. As she continued toward the river, she heard a group of five women discussing the threat. One said, "We are leaving tomorrow morning." A few families were already taking down their lodges. Courage Walks asked where they were going, and was told they were moving anywhere upriver – to get away from the curse of the trading post. Confusion and panic reigned throughout the camp of more than one hundred and thirty lodges.

Courage Walks turned back to the lodge of her friend Two Star. The women had no idea how this disease was spread. They discussed how a person might contract the disease, and what should be done if a person did get it. They agreed the only way to avoid the evil was to move away from the trading post.

Neither had the slightest knowledge that they had already been exposed to the evil, as had many others in the encampment by handling the contaminated trade goods.

Looking Glass Hand was unloading wood from the travois when her mother arrived back at the lodge. "Mother! Mother! Are we moving today? I see many people taking down their lodges. Did father return to show us where the buffalo are located?"

"No, my child, we are not moving our lodge just yet. However, I have decided that you must go away from this place. You will go with your father's cousin Stand Rock and his family. I have spoken to his wife, Bright Day, and she said they are happy you will accompany them."

"Mother, why do I have to go with them? I want to wait for father to come back. Then we can move."

"No, my daughter – it is too dangerous. The smallpox evil is here, and you must get away. I will wait for the return of your father, then we will also move. Now, pack your sleeping robe and clothes on the travois and go to Stand Rock's lodge. Your father and I will follow you soon."

When Looking Glass Hand arrived at the location of the lodge of Stand Rock, the structure had been taken down, folded, loaded on the lodge poles, and hooked to a horse. The family was ready to leave. They planned to travel to the mouth of the Milk River, about five days' journey. For now they just wanted to get as far away from the evil as possible. Though the drizzle had increased to a steady chilling rain, they planned to travel until the last light, make a temporary camp, then continue their journey the next day.

In her lodge, Courage Walks packed most of the family's

items except one cooking pot and the sleeping robes. She hoped Turn Around Walk would return the next day, so they could pack the lodge and join their daughter and the others at the mouth of the Milk River. Courage Walks went to the lodge of Two Star, whose husband had returned from the fort. He said that the white man with the disease had died, and the chief, the council, and the soldiers had decided that the entire encampment would move the following morning.

On the way back to her lodge, Courage Walks heard children crying. A woman screamed. Though light was fading, several more families were leaving, some without their belongings.

The next morning the cold soaking rain continued to fall. Courage Walks and Two Star worked together to take down their two lodges. By the time they had their possessions loaded on horses, more than half of the encampment had begun to move west. Courage Walks and the family of Two Star moved with them. Not everyone was leaving. Some members of the band concluded that the threat was false and decided to remain near the trading post.

The steady rain and mud made the movement toward the mouth of the Milk River slow and torturous. By early afternoon, many families in the procession decided that they had removed themselves far enough from the evil. They stopped near the edge of the Missouri River and set up their lodges. Most planned to continue westward when conditions improved.

Courage Walks and the family of Two Star continued their journey until the daylight began to fade. They set up a temporary camp on the north slope of the valley in a spot where the rainwater would drain rapidly.

By the time they had the shelters in place, the rain had stopped. They could see the red sky in the west as the sun set. Everyone was chilled and wet, but were thankful that tomorrow would be warm with no rain. As she built a fire, Courage Walks thought about her daughter. Was she safe? Had Turn Around Walk also been traveling all day in the rain? Was he back at the trading post?

The following day was warm and clear. The group made good progress, despite being hindered by the soft muddy ground from the two days of soaking rain. Still it would take them at least one, and possibly two extra days to reach the mouth of the Milk River. Courage Walks wondered if the group with which her daughter was traveling had made better progress.

The traveling was better during the next two days. It looked like they would reach their destination by the next evening, and Courage Walks would be reunited with her daughter. Turn Around Walk should not be more than a day behind. While setting up camp that evening, Two Star complained of back pain. It must be caused from the journey.

The following morning, Two Star was still in pain and was not able to load her family's possessions on their horses. Courage Walks hooked the travois to one horse and loaded packs for her friend. She also helped Two Star on the travois where she lay down. With several other families traveling in the group, they again began moving west. There was a slight breeze coming from the west, and the day promised to be warm. Progress would be excellent now that the ground had dried from the rain.

When the sun reached the zenith, the group stopped for a midday meal.

Two Star was no better. Her back pain was severe, and also her head was aching. She had to be helped from the travois. As Courage Walks helped her friend slowly stand up, she touched the skin of Two Star. It felt hot, as if she had been too near a fire for a long time.

It was only under unusual circumstances that a married woman spoke directly to another woman's husband. Courage Walks went to the husband of Two Star after he had watered and picketed the horses to feed on some lush grass. She told him of the condition of his wife. He went immediately to her. The pain and fever had not subsided. Two Star was barely audible when she suggested that they make camp, and spend the afternoon and night at the spot. Surely by tomorrow, she said, she would be recovered from the pain and fever.

Camp was set up and Courage Walks began gathering wood near the river. Each time she bent to pick up wood, she felt a pain in her stomach. Also, her head began to give her pain. After she made a fire, she brought water from the river and bathed the hot face and arms of her friend.

The husband of Two Star rode to another family camp and found an herb doctor, who gave him some medicine to reduce the fever of his wife. Courage Walks made a tea from the herbs. She had to hold up her friend's head to let her sip the medicine. Two Star had not improved by nightfall, and could not eat or drink. Courage Walks covered her with a robe and lay down next to her good friend. Had Two Star contracted the evil from the trading post? If so, how? Did the evil follow them?

Courage Walks slept very little that night because the pain in her stomach became worse, and her head throbbed. She hoped that Turn Around Walk would find them the next day.

She prayed that Looking Glass Hand was safe. As the sun began to rise, Courage Walks looked at her friend. She screamed when she saw that Two Star lay dead. She had hemorrhaged blood from her nose and mouth. She then knew that the white man's evil had caught them – and that she too would die.

The husband of Two Star came, saw his wife, and wept. He rolled her in a robe and tied the ends with strings of rawhide. He told Courage Walks that he would take his wife and lash her body high in a cottonwood tree as was the Nakota custom.

By late afternoon, Courage Walks knew that it would not be long until she too would perish. The strong cool breeze from the west felt good against her feverish skin. The husband of Two Star had not returned. She wondered why, but could not have known that while he was tying the bundle of his wife in the tree, he too had suffered a severe attack of abdominal pain caused by the evil. He lost his footing and fell, breaking his neck on a limb on the way to the ground. He was dead a short time later.

Courage Walks whispered a prayer. "Please protect my child, my daughter, Looking Glass Hand ... and my husband, my love." A gust of wind came up and blew away some of the camp's belongings. The last thing she saw sailing past on the wind as she began to hemorrhage was the calico cloth of Two Star which she had admired.

CHAPTER 22

The four buffalo scouts returned to the trading post the evening after the rain stopped. They had been gone for five days. As they topped the northern slope of the Missouri valley, they could see that only a few lodges were left in the encampment. Even from this distance, Turn Around Walk could see that his lodge was not among those which remained. The scouts anxiously raced their horses the final leg to the nearly abandoned camp.

There was much activity in the camp. Lodges were being taken down and belongings packed. Several men, gathered near the front of one of the few standing lodges, were in deep discussion. The scouts rode up to the men and, without dismounting, asked why only these few lodges remained and why they were being taken down.

The men all began to speak at once. An elder held up his hand. The others stopped talking, and the elder told the story, that a rumor had circulated that one of the white men on the steamboat brought the evil smallpox to the trading post. There had been much confusion. Many families had immediately packed their belongings and left. Others had decided the news was not true and wanted to remain at the post. Later, word came that the man had died. The chief and the council had decided that for the safety of the band, the encampment should move to the mouth of the Milk River. The move had began yesterday morning in the rain.

Continuing, the elder stated that some did not believe the man had died. However, he himself had been to the trading post earlier in the day and was told that the man had died and had been buried last night after the rain stopped. The decision had been made: tomorrow, the remaining lodges would move to the mouth of the Milk to join the rest of the band.

The scouts asked for news concerning their families, but due to the confusion no one could tell them anything. Three of the scouts dismounted and removed the equipment from their horses. Without pause, Turn Around Walk turned his mount and rode directly west into the setting sun.

Turn Around Walk would have ridden west all night long, but knew that his horse had traveled all day through mud. Shortly after sunset, he stopped near the Missouri River bank, unloaded all supplies from the horse, and made a temporary camp. He took the horse to drink from the river, and then picketed the animal so it could feed during the night.

Turn Around Walk could find no dry wood with which to build a fire. However, he gathered enough willow and cotton-wood branches and grass to build a bed above the wet ground. On top of the bed, he placed his buffalo-skin saddle blanket. Here, he sat and ate the last of the pemmican which had been prepared by Courage Walks and packed for him before he left with the other buffalo scouts.

The evening star had been bright in the west since before the horse had been picketed. The other stars were now visible. The westerly breeze had stopped before the sun had set, and now the only sound that could be heard was that of the Missouri River waters, ever moving to the east. The sky was completely clear. The northern lights began to dance. The man lay back on the crude bed and stared into the heavens. Surrounded by the infinite beauty of the night, his thoughts were only of his wife and child.

Where were they? Were they safe? Was the evil visited upon them? Would he ever see them again? He held his medicine bag and prayed that his guardian spirit protect his family.

As the sky brightened in the east, Turn Around Walk awakened from a long night of little sleep. He had nothing to eat, but felt no hunger. He took his mount to the river to drink, then packed his few belongings and put the buffalo saddle blanket on the animal. Upon this he laid the saddle, a pad made from two layers of thick buffalo skin, onto which stirrups were attached. It was held in place by a girth also made of buffalo hide. He tied his possessions behind the saddle, mounted, and rode west.

Before the sun reached the zenith, Turn Around Walk came upon a family encampment of four lodges located near the river bank. He was greeted by the men and learned that they were among some of the last to leave the trading post. They had no information concerning his family. He had not dismounted, but was asked to stay and eat with them. He apologized and told them that he must continue the search for his family.

By mid-afternoon, Turn Around Walk had reached the mouth of Big Muddy Creek where it empties into the Missouri. He had not eaten since the night before, and hunger made his stomach ache. He thought of looking for sagegrouse or other small animals. Riding into the stream, he let his horse take a drink. While the animal was drinking, the man spotted a beaver a short distance upstream. He slowly removed his gun, took aim, and shot the animal. His horse, startled by the explosion of the rifle, lunged into the water, but the man quickly brought him under control.

A short time later a small fire was burning, the beaver was butchered, and the meat, cut into thin strips, was cooking from the end of a willow branch. Hunger gone, the man packed the remaining meat, mounted, and began to move toward the late afternoon sun.

He immediately noticed that the horse was limping on its right hind leg. It must have been strained when the animal had lunged. Turn Around Walk dismounted, removed his belongings, and picketed the horse. He would camp for the night at the stream and begin again the next day. Two more days' travel should bring him to the mouth of the Milk River.

At first light, Turn Around Walk awoke. He led his horse, which was still limping, to the stream for water. He then made a fire and cooked more of the beaver. After eating he packed his belongings, loaded them onto the horse, and began his journey west on foot, leading the animal. Walking would take longer, but the anxious man could not remain stationary.

He walked all day, following the trail of the band on the move ahead of him. He camped near the river that night. The horse still limped, but seemed to be recovering. By late morning the next day, Turn Around Walk had reached the Poplar River where it met the Missouri. After allowing his horse to drink, the man ate some leftover beaver meat and continued walking westward, leading his mount.

In the late afternoon, the outline of two lodges could be

seen toward the sun, which was low in the sky. Though tired, Turn Around Walk excitedly moved at nearly a trot toward the lodges.

No cooking fire smoke could be seen. There was no human activity. Not even the everpresent dogs appeared. Where were the inhabitants? Why had they abandoned their lodges? As he came nearer, he could see several magpies setting on the top of the lodge poles. Others were on the ground near the lodge entrances. He could see in the distance a coyote loping away from the small camp.

The man tied the reins of his horse to one of the stakes which anchored one of the lodges. He peered through the lodge opening, but knew by the scent that the inhabitants were dead before he saw the bodies of the two children and a woman.

It was the evil. He walked the few steps to the other lodge. It too exhibited the strong scent of death. Two men – one sitting against a backrest, the other lying on a robe – were dead. Turn Around Walk knew by instinct that he must not enter the lodges or touch any of the possessions.

He continued the journey west. He had not traveled far before he came across the bodies of a man, a woman, and a baby. The bodies had not only decomposed, but magpies, crows, and coyotes had eaten much of the flesh. These were probably the other inhabitants of the lodges which he had just passed. They were apparently trying to escape the evil when they died.

Turn Around Walk traveled until dark. He camped on the bank of the Missouri. After watering and picketing his horse, he struck a fire, but had no appetite and could not eat. Sitting by the fire, he thought of what he had seen. Had the same thing happened to his family? Would he find them dead tomorrow also? He felt ill in his stomach.

The sun arose with brilliant red rays slicing through the few clouds on the eastern horizon. The man threw off his buffalo robe, but saw none of the beauty of the morning. Leading his horse to the river to drink, he noticed the animal did not limp. He thought of starting a fire, but was not hungry and did not feel the cold. The man packed his belongings, saddled the horse, and rode west at a leisurely trot.

Before midday, Turn Around Walk stopped and let his mount drink from the river. He ate the last of the beaver meat, then continued the journey westward, into a strong breeze. He had traveled only a short distance when he saw the remnants of another camp. Lodge poles and possessions were strewn about. From a distance he could see at least one body.

As he approached the body, his horse could smell the decaying flesh and tried to turn away. The man urged the animal forward. Most of the flesh had been removed from the body by coyotes, magpies, and crows. He could not determine if it was male or female. It was another victim of the white man's evil.

Turn Around Walk began to urge his mount forward, but saw a flash of sunlight reflected from an item on the ground. He pulled up his horse and dismounted. He picked up a knife and examined it. He knew immediately that it was the old and worn knife of Courage Walks.

He looked at the emaciated body and said aloud, "My beautiful wife, the one with the laughing eyes. Mother of my child … my love." The man squatted on his haunches, and tears flowed. His mind went back to that time long ago when he had first met the sad twelve-year-old girl. It was shortly after the death of her parents and brother.

He remembered vividly when he had last seen her, before leaving on the buffalo scouting trip. She had stroked his hand, kissed and embraced him. If only he could embrace her now. How could he live without her?

And where was their daughter Looking Glass Hand? Was she dead also? If so, where was her body? Had it been carried off by animals? This he doubted. He could not believe that she too was dead. He removed his medicine bag and prayed to his guardian spirit and asked that his daughter be protected.

It was some time before Turn Around Walk stood and put the old knife in his belt. His cheeks were stained with dried tears. He knew what must be done.

The man turned and saw his horse grazing a short distance away to the west. He walked to the animal, removed from the pack the buffalo robe he used for sleeping, and laid it beside the body. He then retrieved one of the lodge poles he had seen during his approach to the camp. Using the pole, he carefully moved the remains of his wife onto the robe, making sure to touch nothing with his hands. He rolled the body into a bundle, and tied the ends of the robe securely. He then loaded his wife onto his horse for her final journey.

Turn Around Walk led the horse toward the river. There he found a cottonwood tree. He lashed the body of his loved one into the tree, high above the reach of any animals. As he sat on a limb, he prayed to his guardian spirit for guidance to find his child. He then climbed down from the tree, mounted his horse, and moved upstream.

The sun was low in the west when Turn Around Walk reached the confluence of the Missouri and Milk rivers. About sixty to eighty lodges were located near where the two rivers joined. Long before he reached the encampment, he could hear songs of lament sung by those mourning their family members and loved ones.

As he approached, he could see that the encampment was not circular and was in disarray. Some lodges had been only partially constructed. Others still lay on the ground where they were to be built. Disorder seemed to be everywhere.

When he reached the edge of the camp, an old woman, whom he recognized as the mother of his friend and fellow buffalo-scout Two Strike, stepped from behind a lodge and held up her hand. She stared and said, "My son, do not ride into this camp. If you do, you will die of the white man's evil."

"I am searching for my daughter Looking Glass Hand. Have you seen her? Is she in this camp?"

"My son, I have not seen your wife or daughter. They were not with us during the trip from the trading post. They may have stayed with the others who refused to come with us."

He did not tell the woman of the death of his wife, but just said, "No, they were not there when we returned from scouting for the buffalo."

"They must have been with some of the ones who moved from the encampment early. Have you seen my son? Is he safe?" Turn Around Walk assured her that Two Strike was safe, and that he and the others were probably on their way to the Milk River.

She told him of the trip from the trading post to the present camp. Several people died during the journey. He could see some of the lodges had been sealed, the dead inside. Many of the other lodges had been abandoned, with families fleeing further west to avoid the evil.

He left the camp of the dead and dying, and continued westward.

Turn Around Walk followed the Milk River until darkness was at hand. He then crossed the river, where he felt safer from the death behind him, and set up camp. He struck a fire for warmth. He had nothing to eat, but had no appetite.

The buffalo saddle blanket was laid on the ground. He started to reach for his pack to remove the other robe he used for cover, but remembered that it was now covering his wife.

Tears in his eyes, the man sat, removed his medicine bag and prayed to his guardian spirit that he would find his daughter safe in the near future. Tomorrow he would ride west. Rolled in the saddle blanket, the man slept fitfully.

CHAPTER 23

In the meantime, Looking Glass Hand traveled with her father's cousin Stand Rock and his wife Bright Day, whom she called uncle and aunt, and their two children, White Calf, aged ten, and The Girl, who was eight years old.

They arrived at the mouth of the Milk River where it enters the Missouri. They were three days ahead of the main band of the Paddlers of the Prairie. Here, they remained overnight, planning to follow the Milk River in a northwesterly direction.

The early spring weather had become warm enough that hordes of mosquitoes attacked the family during the evening hours. For a little relief from the insects, they built a smudge fire from sagebrush. The next morning, they crossed the river and followed the top of the valley to avoid the insects. A strong westerly breeze also helped to keep the mosquitoes at bay.

On the third day after leaving the confluence of the rivers, the family turned due west. In leaving the Milk River valley, they also left the mosquitoes. By late afternoon they crossed Beaver Creek at a point about a half-day's ride south of where it enters the Milk River.

From there they followed the stream toward its source. Four days later they made camp on the banks of Beaver Creek, near the eastern slope of the Little Rocky Mountains.

To his wife, Stand Rock said, "While you and the children set up camp, I will ride toward the mountain and find some fresh meat for our evening meal."

"That would be very nice, my husband. Eating dried meat and berries for the entire trip has made me very hungry for deer meat."

"Uncle! Uncle! Do you think that my mother and father will be here for the evening meal?" asked Looking Glass Hand.

"No, my child, I do not believe that they will be here for several more days. They began the journey much later than we." Stand Rock mounted his horse and rode along the creek toward the mountain. In a short time he spotted and killed a whitetail deer. He dressed the animal, loaded it on his horse, and rode back to the camp. The lodge had been set up, and Bright Day had arranged their belongings by the time Stand Rock returned. The three girls had gathered wood and then had gone off to explore the area.

"My husband, I heard you shoot and knew that you would be back soon. That deer looks fat and will be very tasty. And when I tan the skin it will make a very nice shirt for you."

While they were butchering the deer, Bright Day said, "My husband, I have been very worried about our band and the evil. Do you think they will be safe?"

"My love, I am very afraid that many have perished from the white man's disease. I am especially concerned about Turn Around Walk and Courage Walks, and this I do not want to tell to their daughter. I pray that all are safe."

The children found strawberries growing on a hillside near the stream. Picking and eating one, ten-year-old White Calf shouted, "Berries! They taste very good." They all ate berries and talked about how sweet they were.

In a short while, the three girls' hands and mouths were stained red from the berries. "Let us pick more and take them back to the lodge," said The Girl.

On the walk back, they saw an area where thousands of shooting stars were blooming. Looking Glass Hand said, "Those flowers smell so sweet. Let us pick many and take them back for Auntie. They will make the lodge smell so nice."

As they were moving back to camp after picking the flowers, Looking Glass Hand said, "Look! Down the valley, a rider leading a horse. Hurry, we must tell Uncle Stand Rock." They all ran down the slope to the lodge, shouting that a lone rider was coming up the valley toward the camp.

Stand Rock got his rifle in case the man was an enemy. The man and animals came into view, and he waved his arm. Stand Rock recognized him. It was Two Dogs, a member of their band. As Two Dogs dismounted, Stand Rock welcomed him to their camp and invited him to stay with them.

"The smoke from your fire told me you were here," said the visitor.

Stand Rock asked, "The band ... where are they? Have they moved from the trading post? Did the evil smallpox invade the –?"

He was interrupted by Looking Glass Hand, "My mother and father, have you seen them?" Normally children did not interrupt their elders. However, Stand Rock understood her anxiety and let her speak.

"When I left the trading post, your father had not yet returned from the buffalo scouting trip. I did not see your mother, but I believe that she left with the main band."

"Where is the band now?" asked Stand Rock.

Two Dogs told the story. "They are scattered from the trading post to the mouth of the Milk River, or beyond. Death is everywhere. Old people, men, women, children, babies. Dead! The herb doctors failed. The medicine men failed. Nothing seems to stop this great evil which was brought by the white men in the steamboat. Bodies are scattered all along the river valley."

He continued in despair, "Because of the dying, there is no one to properly take care of loved ones. Few have been raised into the trees. The people who have not died have gone to be with their relatives in other bands. I am going to visit my relatives in the Missouri River Dog Band."

"They are dead! Mother and father are dead," sobbed Looking Glass Hand. Bright Day hugged the girl, as tears also filled her own eyes. Sobbing, the child said, "Mother should have come with us. She would now be safe. Why did she have to stay at that ugly place?"

Bright Day, tears running down her cheeks, said, "Your parents will be fine, my child. You will see when they arrive in a few days." With her arm around the shoulders of Looking Glass Hand, she guided the girl into the lodge. The other children followed.

As Bright Day and the three children entered the lodge, Two Dogs asked, "What are you and your family planning to do now?"

"We will go and visit some of my relatives in the Little Rock Mountain Band. We will stay with them until the evil is gone."

The next morning the visitor left to find the Missouri River Dog Band.

Two days later, Stand Rock and family joined the lodges of the Little Rock Mountain Band gathered on the northwest side of the island-like mountain.

CHAPTER 24

Turn Around Walk awoke before dawn. His stomach ached because he had not eaten for more than a day. He searched his pack, but found no food. Mounting his horse, he headed west. The sun, as it came over the eastern horizon, turned the entire western sky a beautiful red color which was hardly noticed by the man.

However, he did notice the new growth of turnips. He dismounted and dug several of the tasty morsels, peeling and eating them as he continued westward. Before the sun reached its high point, the man came across a small flock of sharp-tail grouse. He shot one and cooked it over a small fire. His heart ached and his mind was in turmoil, but with his body nourished, he continued westward in search of his daughter.

Who was his daughter traveling with? Could it be his cousin Stand Rock and his family? If so, were they trying to join the Missouri River Dog band where Stand Rock's wife had relatives? On the other hand, they may have joined the Little Rock Mountain Band where Stand Rock had cousins. Turn Around Walk decided to find the Little Rock Mountain Band. He had to start somewhere.

Two days later, he set up camp less than a full day's ride to the Little Rocky Mountains. The man struck a fire and cooked another grouse he had shot. As he ate, he watched the sun dropping behind the mountains. It was first time since he left the trading post that Turn Around Walk had consciously noticed the setting sun. As it sank slowly, the sky became orange and yellow. Shortly these colors faded into reds and purples.

The infinite beauty of the sky brought a smile to the face of the man. This quickly faded. As young lovers, he and Courage Walks had many times sat on a hill holding hands, watching the sunset fade into darkness. Tears came to his eyes, and he turned away from the beauty and stared into the fire.

The next day, by the time the sun had reached its high point, Turn Around Walk reached the great warm spring where he and his parents had spent a winter in the camp of the grandparents of Courage Walks. He smiled as he thought of the time Courage Walks and the other girls had stolen his clothes and those of the other boys. How the girls had laughed and taunted them to come out of the water! He recalled fashioning his skirt of grass and making a mad dash to the lodge of his parents.

The man picketed his horse. He then removed his clothes and allowed his body to sink into the warm water. As he cleansed his body, he wished that the water could also cleanse some of the pain from his heart and wash away the turmoil in his mind. He prayed that his daughter was safe.

Turn Around Walk stepped out of the pool made by the spring and let the sun dry the water from his body. He then dressed and continued his journey. By evening, he had reached the northwest side of the island mountain and could see smoke from cooking fires rising from the valley of a large stream. He knew he had found the Little Rock Mountain Band and urged his mount into a gallop. As he raced toward the camp of about one hundred lodges, he recognized the lodge of his cousin Stand Rock by its colors.

He eased his horse to a walk. Many people were out doing various chores, and children seemed to be playing everywhere. Turn Around Walk scanned the children, but could not see his daughter. A pain stabbed through his heart. She could be dead.

Turn Around Walk rode to the lodge of his cousin. As he dismounted, Bright Day stepped from the lodge. When she saw him, she smiled, turned back to the lodge opening, and called out, "My husband, your cousin Turn Around Walk has arrived."

"Turn Around Walk, it is so good to have you here," said Stand Rock. "Where is your wife?"

Turn Around Walk turned away and stared at the ground. "My daughter, do you know if she is she alive?"

"Yes, she is here and is alive and well. She misses you and her mother."

"Thank you, my cousin, for protecting her from the evil. Where is she?"

"She and our children went to the stream to get water for cooking. However, knowing them, they are probably playing in the stream. Where is Courage Walks?"

Still staring at the ground, Turn Around Walk, with emotions barely under control, told of finding his dead wife. He also told of all the other casualties that he had witnessed along the way. He said, "It seems that most of our band has died from this evil disease brought to us by the white men. I saw small encampments all along the way from the trading post to the mouth of the Milk River.

"In some of the camps I passed, no one was alive. In others, it appears that most were dead or dying. The evil does not care whom it attacks. Women, children, old people – or soldiers and warriors. It takes everyone. Let us hope that it leaves soon. Or we, like our friends and relatives, will all be dead. If it were to leave today, our band would barely have thirty or forty lodges remaining. I do not know how I am going to tell Looking Glass Hand about her mother." The man stopped talking. He looked at Stand Rock and his wife, who was crying.

"Do you believe that the evil will attack us here?" asked Stand Rock.

"I do not know. It is carried by people, but I do not know how. You cannot see it. From what I have seen, if you touch a person who has the evil, it will come upon you as well. Even if you come into contact with that person's clothes, or other belongings which they have touched, it seems that you can get the disease. It is best to stay away from anyone showing signs of it. I have touched no one. Not even my wife's body." He stared at the ground, remembering how he had used a pole to roll her body onto his buffalo robe.

Looking at her husband, Bright Day said, "Many of the people of our band have relatives and friends in the Little Rock Mountain Band. They may come here, as we did. If they carry the disease, what should we do? Move to the Sweet Grass Hills?"

"My dear wife, let us wait to see if any people come to this band. If so we may need to travel, as you say, to the Sweet Grass Hills," said Stand Rock.

"Have you reported the evil that has struck our band to the chief of this band?" asked Turn Around Walk.

"Yes, I have spoken to the chief. However, we did not know how much destruction had been caused by the evil until you arrived. We must again warn the chief and council, as well as the soldiers. We will speak with them tonight."

"Father, father, you have come at last!" Looking Glass Hand rushed to her father, threw her arms around him, and hugged him. Turn Around Walk put his arm around his daughter and stroked her hair with the other hand.

"Where is mother?" the girl asked. "I know, she is in the lodge." She released her father and dashed into the lodge. She came out almost immediately, and moved slowly toward her father. She stared at him, with tears rolling down her cheeks, and cried, "Mother died! I know that she is dead. I hate her! I hate her! I told her that she should come with us. If she had, she would have been alive and safe now." Sobbing, she stepped into the outstretched arms of her father.

Turn Around Walk held his daughter. Tears welled in his eyes. With a broken voice he said, "Yes, my daughter, the evil has taken your mother. We will now have to live without her."

"How can we live without her? Why did she stay behind? I love her. I love her and miss her."

Bright Day, tears streaming down her face, moved to the child and stroked her hair. "My child, I will now be your mother. You can live in our lodge."

"My wife is correct," said Stand Rock to the girl and her father. "My cousin, you and Looking Glass Hand must live with us in our lodge." Turn Around Walk began to protest, but Stand Rock would hear none of it. "Please give your belongings to my wife, and she will put them in the lodge."

Turn Around Walk continued to hold his daughter. Then he said, "Your mother loved you very much my child, but they are right. We must stay with them for now."

Looking Glass Hand turned and looked at Bright Day, who put her arms around the child and kissed her cheeks where tears were still flowing. Bright Day said, "Come, my daughter, let us take your father's belongings into the lodge."

Stand Rock said to Turn Around Walk, "Come, let us take your horse for a drink from the stream, before we put him with the other horses in the guarded corral."

When the sun was low in the western sky, Turn Around Walk and Stand Rock went to the lodge of the chief of the Little Rock Mountain Band.

They explained the reason for their visit. The terrible disease which had struck the Paddlers of the Prairie Band at the trading post was without doubt on its way to the band of the chief. The chief quickly called a meeting of the council, the soldiers, elders, medicine man, and herb doctors. When all were gathered, the chief brought out the sacred pipe, and lit the tobacco and sweetgrass mixture. He offered it to the four winds, to the sky, and to the earth. He then said a prayer and passed the pipe to all gathered in the circle.

When all had smoked, the chief asked Turn Around Walk to tell the story of evil and death. The man told what he had seen, including the obvious fact that people who had the disease could pass it to others.

All were silent until he indicated he was finished. Immediately, hushed voices could be heard throughout the lodge. The chief held up his hand and all became quiet. He said, "We are here tonight to decide what we shall do. Does the band remain near these mountains, and take a chance that the disease will not reach us? Does the band move north and west to the Sweet Grass Hills, where the evil may not reach us? Or should the band move east and try to help those who are dying of the evil? Who will speak first?"

Spirit Water was first to speak. "My grandfather spoke of a time, long before I was born, when the Little Rock Mountain Band was nearly wiped out by this same terrible evil. It would be best if we moved far from here." As predicted by Bulls Dry Bones at the Medicine Lodge Dance many years ago, Spirit Water, once a weakly child near death, had grown strong and was now chief of the soldiers of the Little Rock Mountain Band.

An elder spoke, "The band should remain here. If people from another band come here, we will not allow them to enter our encampment."

A warrior spoke. "To stop this evil, I will make up a large war party tomorrow. We will travel to the trading post and kill all white men. When this is done, they cannot cause further evil to come upon us." The man continued, "In the future, we must not allow any white men into our territory because they may be carrying the evil. If they come, we must kill all."

Many different views were brought forth. After much discussion, a consensus was reached. The band would remain where they were, near the Little Rocky Mountains. The hunting was very good, and berries would soon be ripe.

Unknown to the group talking things over in the lodge of the chief, while they were meeting, a family of the Paddlers of the Prairie Band entered the encampment to stay for the night in the lodge of relatives. Even the new arrivals did not know that the father was carrying the disease.

CHAPTER 25

Three days after the meeting in the lodge of the chief, news spread that the husband and father of the newest arrivals had died.

The man had first experienced stomach pains the evening he and his family arrived. An herb doctor had been called. She gave the man an herbal drink to reduce stomach pains. The next morning the pain was worse, and the man was burning with fever. He also had back pain and could not rise. The doctor gave him more medicine. Two days later, as a rash began to appear on his body, the man died.

His illness had not been known to the camp until after his death. The news spread rapidly. Some said it was of the disease. Others believed that he had succumbed to an injury.

After hearing of the death, Turn Around Walk and Stand Rock again visited the chief. Turn Around Walk explained that from what he had learned, the fever, stomach pain, and rash indicated the man had died of smallpox. He suggested that the family of the man, and all who had come into contact with them, be separated from the main band to prevent the entire band from getting the evil.

The two cousins left the lodge of the chief. As they walked back to their lodge, they noticed several families taking down lodges and preparing to move. Turn Around Walk said, "It may be well that we move to the Sweet Grass Hills, now that we know the evil has struck this band."

"You are correct, my cousin. We must move today. Let us go and tell our families to begin packing our lodge."

By late morning, with their belongings packed, the family of Stand Rock, with Turn Around Walk and his daughter, left the camp of the Little Rock Mountain Band and traveled north. That evening they made camp along a stream flowing from the Bear Paw Mountains. The next day they would ride to the Milk River, then follow it upstream until they were nearly due east of the Sweet Grass Hills, a grouping of three small mountains which swelled up from the surrounding plains.

On the third day of travel, Turn Around Walk and Stand Rock killed a young buffalo, as they were getting short on meat. The children all cheered and immediately wanted to run to the dead animal and begin butchering. Turn Around Walk motioned them back. He first walked to the animal, touched the head, and gave thanks to the spirit of the animal for giving up its life for the needs of the humans. He then motioned to the children, and they came running.

White Calf and The Girl were given knives by their mother. Looking Glass Hand looked at her father. "Father, may I use your knife?"

Turn Around Walk said, "My daughter, I have something for you." Turning to his horse, from his pack he removed an object wrapped in buckskin. He looked at his daughter. "This is a gift from your mother," he said, and handed the object to her.

Surprised, the girl took the object. "A gift from my mother.

How can that be? She is dead."

She slowly unwrapped the small package. Tears came to her eyes. "This knife ... it is mother's." She hugged her father. Clutching the knife to her body, she said, "Thank you. Thank you. Now I have something by which I will always remember her."

As he watched Looking Glass Hand using the old worn knife, Turn Around Walk thought of its story. The old knife linked daughter to mother. It would always remind Looking Glass Hand – and him – of the tragic death of Courage Walks at the hands of the invisible sickness of the white man. It also linked the young girl to her grandparents – to the violent death of her grandmother, Spotted Leg, and her beloved husband, Rides With Broken Leg, at the hands of the longtime enemies of the Nakota, the Crow.

At the same time, the knife connected the Nakota to their brothers, the buffalo. It bound them to the ever-turning circle of life, to the natural world of their home on the great plains – undulating with tall grasses and flowers, laced with creeks and streams flowing into clear rivers, dotted with the rising oases of the Little Rocky Mountains, the Bear Paw Mountains, the Sweet Grass Hills. On the plains, life was entwined with death. It had been and always would be.

But would their way of life persist? Would the Nakota always ponder the dreams of their guardian spirits? Would they listen in awe for the trumpet peal of the Thunderbird, the emissary of Wahkonda? Would they always follow the buffalo?

Turn Around Walk remembered his wife telling the story of her father, Rides With Broken Leg, when Rides was only a small child. A white trader called Young Curly had come to their camp on the Missouri River. Few in the camp had ever seen a white man before. But the young Rides, only four years old, had bravely gone and sat on the lap of the visiting trader, who had solemnly received the child's presentation of a fox skin, and then had played with the young child.

Since that time long ago, the number of whites in their territory had multiplied many times. They had built forts and had many men and guns to defend them. The buffalo were hunted and slaughtered by the whites moving through Nakota territory. Could the Nakota survive? If they did, how would they and the whites live together?

Turn Around Walk watched his daughter and thought about many things.

Working together, the family finished butchering the young buffalo. Afterward they pitched camp. Bright Day cooked a large meal. Later they all sat and watched the sun set. As the sun disappeared over the horizon, Stand Rock suggested the children turn to the east, where they were delighted to see a nearly full moon rising. Tomorrow, he told them, they would reach their destination.

The next afternoon the group set up camp on the banks of Sage Creek, near the northeast side of the Sweet Grass Hills. Five days later, three families from the Little Rock Mountain Band joined them. They had left the camp two days after the news of the smallpox death. They told of the panic and confusion which had stricken the camp, as others tried to escape the evil.

Turn Around Walk and Stand Rock had discussed the possibility of attending the annual Medicine Lodge Dance. The Paddlers of the Prairie Band had been invited to participate in the ceremony with the Little Rock Mountain Band.

"We probably should stay away from the celebration this year," said Turn Around Walk.

"I believe that we should wait to hear whether the evil has passed," said his cousin Stand Rock.

That is where the matter was left. During the next weeks, several other families joined the group camped on Sage Creek.

All of the families had lost relatives to the disease. They also reported that the evil had not subsided, but was spreading to many other bands of the Nakota, and had also invaded many of the surrounding nations. The decision was made to stay for a while near the Sweet Grass Hills. All in their little group seemed strong and healthy. The hunting was good. Buffalo were plentiful, as well as deer and birds.

Late one afternoon in late summer, Looking Glass Hand, her adopted mother Bright Day, and The Girl were tanning buffalo hides.

As they worked, Bright Day glanced at Looking Glass Hand and remembered out loud: "It was thirteen summers ago when you were born. I remember very clearly. It was late summer, near Woody Mountain, several days after a buffalo hunt. Your mother and I were tanning hides when she felt the pains. A short time later, you were born. You were beautiful."

Looking Glass Hand, now maturing into a woman, had learned all the skills necessary for later in life. What she had not learned from her mother, before she died, had been taught to her by Bright Day. "Do you think that I will ever have a baby of my own?" asked Looking Glass Hand, as she scraped the flesh from the hide.

Smiling, Bright Day looked up from her work, "Oh, yes, my daughter. You will be married, and will have beautiful children some day soon."

"It may be that the white man's evil has killed all the young men of our nation. We have not seen any this entire summer."

Nine-year-old The Girl spoke up, "Who would want to marry a boy anyway?"

Bright Day changed the subject, "Within a few days we are going to leave this area and travel to Fort Union to sell our robes, and get a few supplies for the winter. The men need ammunition also. We may see some of our relatives and friends, if they survived the evil."

Several days later, the small encampment of a dozen lodges was packed, and the group began their journey east. The weather was pleasant, and the prevailing westerly wind seemed to push them on their way. The group followed the Milk River downstream toward the Missouri. Along the route they began to see abandoned camps, with belongings and bones scattered everywhere along the valley, sad evidence of death and destruction caused by the evil.

To avoid the depressing sights, Turn Around Walk moved the group north out of the valley, and they traveled parallel to the stream. They returned to the stream only to obtain water for the animals when none was available on their new route.

Late one afternoon, Turn Around Walk stopped his horse, turned, and pointed into the Missouri River valley. In the far distance the trading post could be seen, with smoke from cooking fires curling above the buildings. They had expected to see lodges near the post, but none were present.

The decision was made to camp near the river for the night. "Tomorrow, Stand Rock and I will ride to the trading post and make inquiries. If the evil is no longer at the white man's trading post, we may move our camp nearer," said Turn Around Walk.

The next day, Turn Around Walk and Stand Rock learned that the evil no longer existed at the trading post, but they also learned that the disease had spread to surrounding tribes. Everywhere, their enemies and friends alike were dying. What they could not know was that the disease would continue to decimate the people of the region for several more months. But it seemed like the disease had run its course in the immediate neighborhood.*

The group decided not to move closer to the trading post, but to remain at their present location for several days. The men went to the trading post nearly every day, and brought back enough supplies, including cloth and ammunition, to last the whole winter ahead. The days were getting shorter, and frost could be seen nearly every morning.

The group decided to move the encampment upstream a short distance to a more sheltered area, and there they spent the winter.

Spring arrived early. On a bright sunny day, Turn Around Walk spoke to the men of the camp. "I believe that we should

. . . .

* The smallpox epidemic of 1836-38 caused an estimated 15,000 deaths among the tribes of the Upper Missouri river. Of that number, the Nakota (Assiniboine) lost an estimated 4,000 souls.

move further upstream. We may be able to find more members of our bands. If not, we can hunt buffalo."

"I believe that we should not only move upstream, but should continue to the location where we were last with the Little Rock Mountain Band. We all have relatives there. Let us hope that they are not all dead from the disease," said Stand Rock.

Everyone agreed with him, and the following morning, possessions were packed, and the entire encampment followed the Missouri River upstream. Not in a hurry, the group moved at a steady pace westward. Along the way they killed the game needed to sustain them. And they observed the remnants of many camps where great numbers of their people had died from the evil smallpox, the year before.

On the sixth day, they reached the area where Courage Walks had died. Camp was set up a short distance from the spot. "It was nearby that your mother died, my child," said Turn Around Walk.

"Father, can you show where she died, and where you found the knife?" asked Looking Glass Hand.

"We may not find the exact spot. But I can take you to the tree in which I placed her."

"Can we go now, father?"

"Yes, my child, we can go now. Let us get the horses. It is too far to walk this evening."

They rode upstream along the river. It had been more than a year since her death, but the location of the tree in which Courage Walks rested was burned in the memory of Turn Around Walk. They could still see their own camp downstream from their location.

"There is the tree, my child."

When they reached the tree, Looking Glass Hand slowly dismounted. She moved to the base of the tree and looked up. With tears streaming down her face, she said, "Oh! Mother, mother, I miss you so much. I wish you could have come with us when we left the trading post. You would still be alive. I love you, mother! I love you!" She put her head down and hugged the base of the tree.

"She hears you, my child." Turn Around Walk had also dismounted and came to the base of the tree. He put his arms around his daughter. She turned to him and hugged him. With tears in his eyes he said, "I miss her too, and I love her even though she is no longer with us."

With arms still around each other, they moved a few paces back from the tree. "Look up, my child. You can see that your mother rests peacefully in the strong robe." For some time, they both looked at the robe which covered the one they loved.

"It is getting late. Let us go look for the place where I found the knife."

"Is it far from here, father?"

"No, my child."

They mounted their horses. Looking Glass Hand guided her horse to the tree. She touched the bark, looked up one last time, and with tears staining her cheeks, they rode away.

They moved north away from the river. After only a short time, Turn Around Walk said, "I believe I can see the spot where last year your mother left her knife for you."

"Oh, father, do you think that there is anything else that mother may have left?"

"I do not know, my child. But we can look."

When they arrived at the site, they dismounted and searched the ground for mementos, but nothing remained except some weather-worn lodge poles. Disappointed and grief-stricken, father and daughter rode in the twilight back to the encampment.

The next day the group reached the confluence of the Milk River. Bright Day, Looking Glass Hand, and The Girl were setting up the lodge when The Girl said, "Look! Up the river, many people are coming. Mother, do you think that any of them will be from our band?"

"I do not know, my child. It appears they are Nakota. But I cannot see if they are from our band. There must be at least one hundred people in the group."

Turn Around Walk, Stand Rock, and four other men rode out to meet the newcomers, and invited them to set up camp near their own camp. The entire group was from the Little Rock Mountain Band. From them they learned that the Paddlers of the Prairie Band were still invited to attend the Medicine Lodge Dance which was to take place this year near the Little Rocky Mountains.

The new arrivals began unloading their possessions and lodges. Looking Glass Hand, curious, began walking in the direction of the beginnings of the new encampment. She had nearly reached the area when she heard The Girl calling her name. She turned to see her adopted sister coming toward the new camp.

Looking Glass Hand smiled, then heard a shout and pounding hooves behind her. As she turned to see the cause of the commotion, someone hit her from the side, throwing her about three or four paces to her right.

A heartbeat later, a horse, which had panicked after being tangled in a rope, galloped past her.

Stunned from the blow, Looking Glass Hand lay on her side, trying to catch her breath. She heard a male voice asking, "Are you injured? Can I help you to stand?" She also heard shouting, and people rushing to her.

"Sister! Sister! Are you hurt?" Looking Glass Hand slowly turned, looked up, and saw The Girl bending over her.

Still weak, she tried to sit up. "What ... what happened? How did I ...?" She felt a strong pair of hands gently lift her to her feet. Slowly she turned and stared into the eyes of a handsome youth who appeared to be two or three years older than she.

"Sister! Sister! He saved your life. Had he not pushed you aside, the horse would have trampled you." The Girl stepped between the two and hugged her adopted sister. Looking Glass Hand felt the hug, but saw only the face of the stranger who had lifted her from the ground.

"I hope that I have not hurt you," said the stranger. "My name is Step On Earth."

"Her name is Looking Glass Hand," said The Girl, nearly shouting. She had released her adopted sister, who still had said nothing.

"I will be fine soon," said Looking Glass Hand, after a few silent moments had passed. "You did not injure me. I lost my breath for a short time. My sister said that you saved my life. How can I thank you?"

A crowd had gathered around them, but the young couple saw no one except each other.

"There is no need to thank me. I am happy to have been of

help."

The concentration of the young couple on each other was broken by the arrival of Bright Day. "My daughter! My daughter! What happened? Were you hurt? Your face and hands have dirt clinging to them. What happened?"

"I am not sure what –"

The Girl cut her off and excitedly told the story of the near tragedy and rescue to her mother and the surrounding crowd.

Bright Day looked at the youth and said, "Thank you, my child, for saving the life of my daughter. Where is your mother? I would like to thank her, and your father also."

The eyes of Step On Earth dropped to the ground, and with a catch in his voice, he said, "Both are dead from the white man's evil."

She reached out and touched his arm and said, "I am very sorry to hear about your parents. This evening you shall come to our lodge and eat with us. We have fresh buffalo meat, and will celebrate what you have done for my daughter. Our lodge is the one on the north side of our camp. Come, girls, we have much work to do."

Bright Day moved into the crowd, which had begun to disperse, with The Girl following.

Step On Earth turned back to Looking Glass Hand who was staring at the ground. He gently put his fingers beneath her chin and lifted her head. She had tears in her eyes. "What is wrong? Do you still have pain?"

Choking back sobs, the young woman said, "The only pain I have is in my heart – which I feel every day and night since father told me that mother had died from the disease."

"But your mother was here."

"That is my adopted mother. I love her very much, but it is not the same."

He put his arms around her, held her and said, "I am very sorry for you. I understand the pain. It never seems to go away." They stood nearly motionless for a short time looking into each other's eyes.

"I must go now and help my adopted mother."

As she left, the young man held out a hand toward her. "I will see you this evening." Before she turned to leave she looked at him, and he saw tears in her eyes. She made a sign of goodbye and was gone.

After the evening meal was finished, Turn Around Walk, Stand Rock, and Step On Earth visited until well after the sun had set. "It is getting late, I must go," said Step On Earth as he rose to leave. "I thank your wife for the meal. It was very good to eat fresh buffalo meat again."

"You must come again," said Stand Rock.

"I must feed the dogs and change the wind flap. I can smell smoke in here," said Looking Glass Hand as she moved to the lodge entrance and was gone.

Step On Earth took leave and stepped outside. Looking Glass Hand was waiting behind the lodge. She touched his hand and whispered, "I thank you for saving my life. I must go back into the lodge now. My parents will soon miss me." He ran his fingers through her hair and left.

The next morning the entire camp was filled with the activity of preparing to move. The newcomers would move east to the trading post where they would spend several days before returning to the Little Rocky Mountains. Turn Around Walk, Stand Rock, and their group would continue their trip west.

As the newcomers began moving east, Looking Glass Hand frantically tried to find Step On Earth in the crowd. She heard his voice before she saw him riding directly at her.

"The Medicine Lodge Dance. We will meet there." He leaned down and touched her cheek. Then he turned his horse and rode away.

The young woman stared after him. She whispered, "Yes, we will meet there."

EPILOGUE

Looking Glass Hand and Step On Earth eventually married, and had one child, Four Legged Stone, who was born in 1843. They continued the nomadic existence of the Nakota, roaming between present-day Canada and eastern Montana.

Four Legged Stone married and had six children, one of whom was Brown Hair, grandmother of the author.

In 1921, Four Legged Stone was interviewed by the Bureau of Indian Affairs for enrollment on the Fort Belknap Reservation, Montana. From this interview, the author was able to trace his ancestry back to Turn Around Walk, who was born about 1805.